Book Three

EPIC ZERO 3

Tales of a Super Lame Last Hope

By

R.L. Ullman

But That's
Another Story...
Press

Epic Zero 3: Tales of a Super Lame Last Hope
Copyright © 2016 by R.L. Ullman.

EPIC ZERO is a TM of R.L. Ullman

All rights reserved. This book or any portion thereof may not be reproduced or used in any manner whatsoever without the express written permission of the publisher except for the use of brief quotations in a book review.

Cover design by Yusup Mediyan
All character images created with heromachine.com.

Published by But That's Another Story... Press
Ridgefield, CT

Printed in the United States of America.

First Printing, 2016.

ISBN: 978-0-9964921-8-8
Library of Congress Control Number: 2016911949

For Sandy and Ken,
thanks for everything

Don't Miss the Epic Adventure!

GET MORE EPIC!

Grab a FREE copy of
Epic Zero Extra only
at rlullman.com

TABLE OF CONTENTS

ONE

I SCREW UP BIG TIME

I've totally got this creep in the bag!

The only thing standing between us is a lousy manhole cover, and once I crack this puppy open he's all mine! I stick my fingers in the holes and yank, but the only cracking I hear comes from my back! I let go and stretch my spine. Wow, that thing is heavier than Dog-Gone after a buffet lunch.

I'm going to need leverage to lift this sucker up. Well, I guess the only good thing about standing in a disaster zone is there's plenty of options. I grab a severed pipe and shove it into the pick hole. Pushing down with all my might, the manhole pops open like a bottle cap. I drop the pipe, snatch the metal disc with both hands, and roll it to the side.

A rotten stench floods out of the opening straight into my nostrils. As tempting as it is to turn away, I can't—not when there's justice to be served! Pinching my nose, I crouch down at the edge, ready to drop into the dark abyss otherwise known as the Keystone City sewer system.

All I need to do is jump.

But… I can't.

And what's worse, I know why.

Maybe I should rewind. The trouble started an hour ago. I was hanging with my family on the Waystation, watching reruns of old sitcoms when the Meta Monitor started blaring: "Alert! Alert! Alert! Meta 3 disturbance. Repeat: Meta 3 disturbance. Power signature identified as Alligazer! Meta 3 disturbance. Power signature identified as Alligazer!"

Popcorn flew everywhere as we leaped into action. I can still hear Dad's voice as we boarded the Freedom Flyer. "Remember, Freedom Force," he warned. "Alligazer is big trouble."

Look, I'm not saying Dad's wrong. I mean, I'd never faced Alligazer myself but I knew all about him. After all, his ugly mug was posted at the top of our Meta Most Wanted List. With big, yellow eyes, and teeth sharper than Ginsu knives, he had a face only a mother could love.

But I'd probably go a step further than Dad. I'd say Alligazer is more than big trouble. I'd say he's downright lethal.

You see, once we reached the scene of the crime the only part of Keystone Savings Bank left standing was the vault. The rest of the building was gone, as in, completely obliterated. Alligazer had blown it to bits. But that wasn't the worst part.

Not by a long shot.

Despite the massive damage, all these civilians were still hanging around. I couldn't imagine why they didn't run for their lives. So, I went up to one guy to see what his problem was.

And realized he was a statue.

And it wasn't just him. There were dozens more.

All solid, stone statues.

Petrified by Alligazer.

There were police officers, bank tellers, customers. All innocent bystanders who got petrified—forever frozen in fright—never to move again!

I was horrified. Immediately, I turned to TechnocRat. "We've got to save these people! We have to change them back to normal!"

But he just shook his little head and said, "It's not possible. Once they've turned to stone, their blood hardens and stops flowing. I'm afraid they're gone."

I was so outraged—we all were—that I knew we had to catch Alligazer before he could do this to anyone else. But he was nowhere to be found.

Dad suggested we split into search teams to cover more ground. I partnered with Makeshift, but we couldn't find Alligazer anywhere. I suggested Makeshift port to the top of a building to get a more panoramic view. I figured I'd be okay for a few seconds alone.

And that's when I spotted him—two yellow eyes, darting back and forth from beneath a truck. Then, he emerged, big, green, and muscular, dragging a long tail behind him. He was carrying a sack and scampered like lightning to the manhole. He lifted the cover like it was nothing, hopped inside, and closed it behind him.

If I hadn't seen him, he would have gotten away with it. But that wasn't going to happen on my watch.

I briefly considered calling the rest of the Freedom Force, but I figured I could handle it. I mean, I'm part of the team now, and here was my chance to show them how much I've grown. If I could get close enough, I could simply negate his powers. Then, he wouldn't be so dangerous. It all seemed pretty straightforward.

So, why haven't I jumped in to save the day?

Images of those statues flash through my mind: a woman talking on a cell phone, a man looking up from his paper, a police officer heroically drawing her weapon. The only thing they had in common was being in the wrong place at the wrong time. That, and the sheer look of terror on their faces.

I wonder if they felt their skin hardening? Their blood slowing? Their hearts stopping?

Sweat trickles into my eyes and I wipe it away. I'm totally freaked out. But if I don't shake this now, Alligazer will escape. And then he'll do it again.

I've got a job to do—and thanks to Shadow Hawk and TechnocRat—now I've got the tools to do it. After my last adventure, I realized I needed more help in case I got in over my head—which seems to happen with more regularity than I care to admit.

So, they designed a utility belt just for me.

Opening the front, left-side compartment, I pull out a mini-flashlight and clench it in my teeth. Then, I grab the rusty rails of the sewer ladder and begin my descent. Within seconds, I'm swallowed by darkness. Reaching the bottom, I jump off the last rung into ankle-deep, ice-cold sewer water.

Just. Freaking. Wonderful.

The funky smell hits me hard, making my eyes water. I flick on the flashlight and shine it around. The sewer tunnel is damp and gray, with patches of dark moss growing all over. Large, cobweb-covered pipes run along the walls in each direction. The water rushing over my feet is brown and sludgy.

Well, this gets my vote as the creepiest place ever.

Unfortunately, there's no sign of Alligazer. I'm kicking myself for waiting too long! I've got to catch him, but which way should I go?

Just then, I hear squeaky noises to my right. Flashing my light, I catch a pair of gigantic rats running along a pipe attached to the wall. I'm guessing TechnocRat isn't throwing a dinner party. But then I notice they're carrying something in their mouths.

It's money!

From the bank!

Alligazer must have headed that way!

I sprint ahead, but my sloshing feet echo noisily down the tunnel. Well, if he didn't know I'm here, he certainly does now. I shine my flashlight around, hoping to catch a glimpse of the villain before he catches me.

As I get sucked deeper and deeper into the bowels of the sewer, I start second-guessing myself. I mean, maybe I shouldn't be down here on my own. Maybe I should have called the rest of the Freedom Force. Maybe I'm—

"Welcome," comes a deep, slithery voice.

—in serious trouble!

That sounded like it came from in front of me! I aim my flashlight forward, but Alligazer isn't there.

"You're either really brave or really stupid," he says, this time from behind me. "These sewers are my home. You don't stand a chance."

I spin around, but he's not there either. He's too fast!

Suddenly, there's a splash, and my flashlight is ripped clean out of my hand!

"Now you're really in the dark," Alligazer says from yet another direction, his evil laugh reverberating through the sewer.

It's pitch black and I can't see a thing. He's probably standing right in front of me, watching me spin around like a blindfolded fool trying to bash a piñata. I know he can take me out if he wants to, but he's not, which means he's toying with me. He thinks I'm helpless.

The thing is, I'm not.

I dig into my utility belt and pull out a flare. I remove the cap and rub it against the rough surface of the stick. Suddenly, the sewer lights up like the Fourth of July. Now I know why Shadow Hawk never leaves home without one.

I hold the burning flare away from my body and look around. Time to render him powerless. Now, where'd he go?

Just then, I hear a scratching noise over my head.

Uh oh.

He lands on me hard—the force of his body pushing me underwater. My nose scrapes the cement floor, and my mouth fills with sewage. I try getting up, but the floor is so slick I lose my footing and re-submerge. Then, the current grabs me and I feel myself being pulled away.

I reach out for something to stop my momentum, but the pressure is so strong I'm carried away! I find myself going under again and again. It's hard to breathe! I flail my arms out, trying to hook onto something— anything. Finally, I grab a pipe dangling from the wall. My body slams hard into the cement surface and I dig in my heels, catching them on a ridge. Steadying myself, I swing my leg over the pipe, hugging it with everything I've got.

I'm gasping for air, lucky to be alive. Clearly, I'm miles from where I started. And there's no sign of

Alligazer. Then, I realize the only reason I can see at all is because there's another manhole right above my head—and it's open—streaming in sunlight.

Alligazer must have crawled along the ceiling and escaped! I didn't know he could walk on walls. Time to update his Meta Profile. But I'll have to do that later. Right now, I've got to get out of here.

I reach into my utility belt and pull out a grappling gun. Then, I aim at the manhole and fire. The claw-shaped projectile latches onto the rim, stretching the cable taut. I release the trigger, and the cable retracts, pulling my sorry self out of the sewer and towards freedom.

Reaching the surface, I roll back into civilization. I'm lying flat on my back—cold, wet, and reeking like a Porta-Potty. I close my eyes and take in the fresh air.

Well, that was an epic failure.

"Ewww, gross!" a woman cries.

Opening my eyes, I'm surrounded by video cameras.

News cameras.

Fabulous.

"Is that a hero or villain?" some guy asks.

"You know any heroes that smell like that?" another man answers.

"Shut up and keep rolling," a woman says. "Hey, kid, you responsible for all of this?"

Wait. What?

"Did you blow up the bank?"

Are you kidding me?

Suddenly, I'm bombarded with questions. I've got to get out of here, but I'm so wiped I can't move.

"Back off!" comes a familiar voice.

Suddenly, the news reporters part, and Captain Justice strides through the crowd, his golden scales of justice a sight for sore eyes.

"Please, back away," he orders. "Give him space."

He kneels beside me and whispers, "Are you okay?"

"I think so," I whisper back.

"Where the blazes were you?" Dad asks.

"In the sewers. I-I chased Alligazer down there. But he got away."

"You chased Alligazer?" Dad says surprised. "You found Alligazer?"

"Yeah," I answer, my head still woozy. "We had a big fight in the sewer. Hey, did you know there are rats like five times the size of TechnocRat down there?"

"Forget that," Dad says. "Why didn't you call us?"

"I... I don't know," I answer. "I didn't want to lose him. And I wanted to make a difference."

Dad rubs his face with his hands. "Oh, you made a difference alright. But not in the way you were hoping for."

"What are you talking about?" I ask.

"I'm guessing Alligazer popped out of that manhole two minutes before you did," he says.

"Yeah, I figured," I say. "But how'd you know that?"

"It's pretty obvious," Dad says, turning away from me, "because only he could leave behind something like that."

Like what?

I sit up and look over to see what Dad's all worked up about, when I notice another statue.

But it's not just any statue.

It's Makeshift!

TWO

I HANG UP MY TIGHTS

I totally messed up.

So, while the rest of the team loads Makeshift into the cargo hold, I climb into the Freedom Flyer and slump into my chair. I know I should have helped, but I couldn't bear to look at Makeshift's petrified face.

Not after what I've done.

When the team finally boards the jet, no one even looks my way. Instead, they take their places and we rocket home. My eyes are glued to Makeshift's seat. It's empty now, and it's all my fault.

The ride back is awkwardly silent. The team is probably thinking of ways to console me. They'll probably tell me everything is okay—that it was an accident—that these are the risks you take in this line of work.

But I know better.

Makeshift is gone because of me.

Deep down, I'm sure they're wondering if they can trust me. And how can I blame them? I seem to screw up royally over and over again. Who knows who I'll hurt next?

I can already guess what Mom and Dad will say. Despite saving the world twice, they'll tell me I'm still too green for this. They'll tell me I'll be taking a break for a while—a long, long while.

But I won't give them the chance.

As soon as we dock on the Waystation and deboard the Freedom Flyer, I make an announcement. "Ladies and gentlemen, effective immediately I'm retiring from the Freedom Force—for good."

Then, I hand Dad my utility belt and head straight for my room.

"Elliott, wait!" Mom calls after me but I pretend not to hear her.

Dog-Gone pads softly behind me, whimpering the whole way. Don't get me wrong, I appreciate what he's trying to do, but when we reach my room I tell him I need to be alone and shut the door. Then, I peel off my sewer-infested bodysuit, hop into the shower, and ball my eyes out.

I still can't believe what happened. I never thought Alligazer would get away. I never thought Makeshift would be turned to stone. I thought I was doing the right thing—the heroic thing.

But I'm clearly not hero material.

Instead, I'm a hazard—a moving violation—a risk to society. So, I have no choice but to give up caped crusading. For everyone's sake.

Tomorrow, I'll ask Mom to re-enroll me at Keystone Middle School and go back to the ordinary life of a run-of-the-mill 6th grader. No more hunting supervillains. No more putting lives in jeopardy. No more bonehead mistakes.

I towel off and stare at myself in the mirror. My hair is wet and soggy, my eyes red from crying. Yep, starting tomorrow, I'll be your typical anonymous tween-ager.

Instead of heroically responding to Meta alerts, I'll be plowing through homework. Instead of squaring off against supervillains, I'll be dodging bullies. Yep, doesn't that sound just awesome?

Or should I say awful?

I throw on some sweats and flop onto my bed. Awful is right. But this is my new life, so I'd better get used to it. I start counting ceiling tiles when—

BANG, BANG!

There's a knock at my door.

"No one's home!" I shout.

"Hey!" Grace yells. "Open up."

Grace? What's she doing here?

"C'mon, Elliott," she says, knocking again. "Let me

in or I'll get Master Mime to bust it open."

"Fine!" I answer, rolling off my bed. "What do you want?" But I suspect I already know the answer. Whenever I screw up I can always count on Grace to rub my nose in it.

I swing the door open to find her standing there with her arms crossed. Her mask is off, and her blond hair is pulled back in a ponytail. "To talk," she says, striding in and sitting on the end of my bed.

"Well, then," I say, slamming the door shut. "Talk."

"Listen, squirt," she says, "I know you feel horrible about what happened to Makeshift but you can't just give up. You're a superhero—a member of the Freedom Force, for Pete's sake. It's not your fault. Bad stuff like that is just gonna happen."

Hang on. Is she trying to console me?

"Look, you didn't do that to Makeshift," she continues. "That Alligazer creep did."

"But it's *my* fault," I say. "I mean, I didn't call you guys for help when I should have. I thought I could do it on my own. And… I couldn't. I just keep thinking 'what if?' What if I did call for help?"

"Elliott," Grace says. "You could 'what if' yourself to death. Okay, what if you did call us? Maybe this whole thing wouldn't have happened. Or maybe *you'd* be turned to stone right now."

"That'd be fine with me," I mutter. "I deserve it."

"Look," she says, standing up, "there's no how-to

manual on being a hero. In this business, anything can happen. You just have to do what you think is right, and most of the time, it turns out okay. But there's one thing you can't do, and that's give up—especially on yourself."

She lifts my chin with her finger and forces me to look into her blue eyes. "Okay?"

I fake a smile and say, "I'll think about it."

"Great," she says. "But do yourself a favor."

"What's that?"

"Don't watch TV." Then she winks and lets herself out, closing the door behind her.

I start pacing. Look, I appreciate what she's saying, but I really don't think I can do this anymore. I mean, I don't want anyone else to get hurt because of me. And what did she mean by don't watch TV?

Oh, no!

I throw open the door and bolt down the hall to the Lounge. Blue Bolt and Master Mime are relaxing on the sofa with their feet propped up on a leather ottoman.

They're watching the news.

A square-jawed reporter looks straight to camera with a smug expression and says, "And if you've been living under a rock, and haven't seen these images from today's Keystone Savings Bank fiasco, you may want to sit down for this one."

Then, it cuts to an image of Makeshift. He's petrified, his arms blocking his face. A field reporter begins to narrate, "Today, a villain known as Alligazer destroyed Keystone Savings Bank, and turned twenty-five people at the scene into statues—including this superhero who has been identified as Makeshift, an apprentice of the Freedom Force."

Suddenly, the camera pans down to a brown, gloppy mess clinging to Makeshift's stone leg.

"While the Freedom Force were on the scene, they were unable to apprehend Alligazer. However, they did manage to capture his accomplice who emerged from the sewer system."

His accomplice? Who's that?

The camera pans in on the mystery accomplice's dirty face.

Wait a minute! That's me!

"At this time, the identity of the criminal has not been disclosed," the reporter continues. "But those of us in the media are referring to him as 'Stink Bug' because— well, we'll let you draw your own conclusions. It's assumed the Freedom Force have transferred him to Lockdown where—"

"Turn it off!" I yell, startling Blue Bolt and Master Mime.

"Hey there, Stink Bug," Blue Bolt says with a smile.

"Not funny," I snap.

"Whoa, sorry," Blue Bolt says. "I was just teasing."

Master Mime flicks his wrist and a giant, purple peace sign magically appears.

"Elliott," Blue Bolt says. "You know it's not your

fault, right?"

"Why does everyone keep saying that? Of course it's my fault. It's all my fault!"

But before they can respond, I'm off. I just want to be alone. My stomach rumbles and I realize I haven't eaten in hours. All the food is in the Galley, and I hope no one's around so I can grab a snack and head back to my Fortress of Solitude, otherwise known as my room.

But no such luck.

Shadow Hawk is sitting at the table, polishing off one of his trademark peanut butter and banana sandwiches. "Hey, kid," he says. "Want one?"

"No," I say, salivating. "Well, maybe."

"My pleasure," he says, popping the last bite into his mouth. He rises and heads over to the counter. "How are you holding up?"

"Honestly," I say, leaning against the counter. "Not so hot." Here we go again. The last thing I want right now is more sympathy.

"I understand," Shadow Hawk says, unpeeling a banana. He reaches into his utility belt, flicks open a Hawk-knife, and dices the banana like a master chef. "After all, what happened to Makeshift was your fault."

Wait, what? Did he just say it was *my* fault?

"You were irresponsible," he says, spreading peanut butter onto the bread. "And I expected more from you."

What? I'm taken aback! I'm speechless! Flabbergasted! How dare he! What happened to the sympathy? Doesn't he care how I feel right now?

"What's wrong?" he says, reading my expression. He washes off the Hawk-knife, closes it, and puts it back into his utility belt. Then, he hands me my sandwich. "Being a superhero is a big responsibility. Innocent lives are at stake. Heroes' lives are at stake. I'm not going to sugarcoat it for you, if you don't think you're up for the job, giving up the suit is the right decision."

I swallow hard. I-I don't know what to say.

Then, he puts his gloved hand on my shoulder. "But I've seen you in action. I know you've got what it takes. Listen, real superheroes don't run away from their mistakes. They own up to them so they don't do them again next time. Take some time to think about what you could have done differently. Then, pick yourself up and put on the cape again. But don't wait too long. Got it?"

"Yeah," I say. "I got it."

"Great," he grins.

Suddenly, the Meta Monitor's alarm goes wild, "Alert! Alert! Alert! Meta 2 disturbance. Power signature identified as Blood Sport! Alert! Alert! Alert!"

"Maybe you sit this one out," Shadow Hawk says with a wink.

"Thanks," I say. "And thanks for the sandwich."

"Enjoy it," he says, and then he exits.

I meander through the halls, chewing on both the sandwich and what Shadow Hawk said. It was like a slap in the face, but one I needed. Of course, he's right—he's always right. I mean, all I've ever wanted is to be a superhero. If I'm going to get out there again, I'll need to get over this.

Which means there's something I need to do, no matter how painful it's going to be.

I'm already in the West Wing, so I hang a left and slowly make my way over to an area I'd rather not be—TechnocRat's laboratory.

The white doors slide open, revealing a large, sunken chamber, and my senses immediately kick into overload. Every square inch of the wall is lined with beakers, test tubes, and vials of various sizes and colors. Large, cylindrical chambers run from floor to ceiling, bubbling with strange gaseous substances. Black tables fill the center, covered with microscopes, computer monitors, circuits, and assorted machinery. It's a nerd's paradise.

Needless to say, the disaster that is TechnocRat's laboratory drives Dad batty. TechnocRat loves bringing him in here to help with his experiments and watch him twitch. I know Dad just wants to get a garbage bag and clean everything up, but he can't risk spoiling one of TechnocRat's inventions. It's a funny little game they play. I guess they're like the odd couple of superheroes.

I move past a cart of electromagnetic, worm-like thingies, and head towards the back—to the reason why I'm here in the first place. I find him in the corner hooked up to a network of monitoring equipment.

Makeshift.

I reach out and touch his cold, solid arm. I hate myself for not having the guts to face him before.

Or to apologize.

"Hi, buddy," I say. "Can you hear me?"

I look up at the overhead monitor, but all his vitals are flat-lined. I wonder if he's still in there. If he can hear me somehow, but just can't respond.

"I-I'm sorry," I say, as tears stream down my cheeks. "I didn't know this was going to happen to you. I hope you can forgive me."

But there's no response.

"If you're still in there. If you can hear me, just give me a sign."

WHOOSH!

Instinctively, I duck, as a warm sensation crosses my body. What the heck was that?

I step back and look at Makeshift, but he hasn't budged. Then, I notice something glaring bright outside the porthole.

It's a trail.

A fiery trail!

I follow its path. It looks like it came from deep space—and it's heading straight for Earth!

Then, I realize I've seen a trail like that before, and my heart sinks to my toes.

I know exactly who it belongs to.

The Herald!

Meta Profile

Name: Alligazer
Role: Villain   Status: Active

VITALS:

Race: Human
Real Name: Anton Bing
Height: 6'3"
Weight: 225 lbs
Eye Color: Yellow
Hair Color: Bald

META POWERS:

Class: Energy Manipulator
Power Level:
- **Extreme petrification**
- **Limited super-strength**
- **Limited super-speed**
- **Can cling to surfaces**

CHARACTERISTICS:

Combat	85	
Durability	90	
Leadership	55	
Strategy	69	
Willpower	87	

THREE

I CAUSE AN INTERNATIONAL INCIDENT

I scribble down a note for my parents, grab a fresh costume out of the Equipment Room, tiptoe around a snoozing Dog-Gone in the hallway, and hit the Hangar.

Within seconds, I'm piloting a Freedom Ferry through space, hot on the Herald's trail. So many things are flying through my brain I don't know where to begin. I mean, the last time I saw the Herald, he descended upon a planet named Protaraan, and marked it for destruction by a globe-eating creature called Ravager— the Annihilator of Worlds!

I've been afraid something like this might happen ever since Siphon destroyed Order and Chaos back on Arena World. Once those two cosmic brothers were gone, no one was left to control that planet-gobbling monster. It was only a matter of time before Ravager showed up to destroy someone's world. I just never thought it would be mine!

I mean, recently I learned there are all of these other universes out there! Mirror universes, like the one Grace 2 lives in. And somehow, out of all of those, Ravager has chosen mine.

Why do I have all the luck?

Fortunately, the Herald may be the worst hide-and-seek player of all time. His trail is brighter than the sun. But being easy to track is one thing, catching up to him is quite another. I mean, the guy can really motor!

According to the Freedom Ferry's monitor, I enter Earth's atmosphere somewhere over Asia. I pick up the Herald's path weaving through mountains and then jetting across the ocean. It looks like he's now somewhere over Japan.

As far as I'm concerned, my job is simple. First, catch him. Second, get him off the planet. Seems pretty straightforward. I only see one little hiccup.

I've got no clue how to do that.

Not too long ago I was kidnapped by the Zodiac, a band of alien, teenage vigilantes because they thought I had the Orb of Oblivion—the only object capable of destroying Ravager. Even though I didn't know it at the time, they were right. I did have the Orb. It was buried inside of me. But Siphon pulled it out when he absorbed my powers, and then used it to destroy Order and Chaos. Now the Orb is gone.

And I'm on my own.

So much for early retirement.

I follow the Herald's trail through a cluster of thick clouds, and when I come out the other side, it's clear I won't be chasing him much farther.

Because he's waiting for me.

The heat blast comes fast and furious. I try to pull up, but it catches my left wing full-on, bursting it into flames. I activate the exterior cooling jets to extinguish it, but when the foamy liquid clears, my wing is still burning! Whatever he's hit me with isn't standard-issue fire! And the flames are creeping towards the cockpit!

My sensors are going nuts, so I check the radar to find even more bad news.

He's on my tail!

I spin the Freedom Ferry as another heat blast shoots over my right wing. I've got to lose this creep and fast! But how? I'm a sitting duck in the open sky.

Looking below, I see a giant expanse of water—wonderful fire-extinguishing water.

I push the yoke forward and nose drive straight for the ocean, switching the Freedom Ferry to amphibious mode. Then, I brace myself for impact.

SPLASH!

The Freedom Flyer knifes through the water, diving deep so he can't spot me from the air. I check the radar again and this time there's no sign of the Herald. I've lost him! Whew!

Then, I check my wing, fully expecting the fire to be snuffed out, but it's not! Giant flames are still crackling away! But how's that possible?

Suddenly, I'm blinded by an intense burst of light. Instinctively, I hit the brakes. What's going on? For a few seconds, all I see are spots, but when my vision clears I'm faced with something I'm not expecting.

Floating five feet in front of my ship is the Herald! He's breathing underwater and still very much on fire.

If I don't beg for mercy I'm cooked! I scan the control panel and flip on the external communications system. But before I can speak, I hear—

"I know you, little one."

I look up to find him staring at me—studying me— his arms folded across his chest. Then, I realize I'm only seeing him because he's lowered his intensity. He's big and broad-shouldered, but his facial features are impossible to see through the dancing flames. All I can make out are pointy-ears and a crooked nose.

"Y-You do?" I reply nervously.

"Yes," he says, his voice crackling like a campfire. "You battled on Arena World. You were there for the final battle before everything disintegrated. You were one of the so-called heroes. A little hero."

All this 'little' talk is making my blood boil.

"And you're a minion," I shoot back. "For Ravager!"

The fire man laughs. "So, you know of Ravager. And soon, Ravager will know of you. And your world."

Wait? Did he just say *soon*? Does that mean Ravager doesn't know about us yet? I've still got a chance!

"Why don't you get lost," I say. "While you still can."

"Is humor your superpower?" he says. "I suppose in the end, it does not matter. Your fate is sealed." He looks upwards. "My job is to find fertile planets for Ravager to consume. But I fear this has become more difficult. Without Order and Chaos, the multiverse is collapsing. Whole galaxies are vanishing in the blink of an eye, taking all of their planets with them. But I could tell from deep space that your galaxy is not yet affected. Yours is one of the stable ones. Yours is free of the Blur. At least, for now."

"Blur? What are you talking about?"

"I have wasted enough time with you," the Herald says. "Ravager must feed."

He's going to take off! I've got to stop him! I can't let him get away and lead Ravager here!

I'm not sure the Freedom Ferry's weapons are powerful enough to affect him. But I've got something better. I've got Meta powers!

I only hope it's enough.

I concentrate hard and wash my negation powers all over him. Suddenly, his bright, orange flames flicker and then blow out like a candle.

It worked? It worked!

"What is happening?" he says.

Now I've got to reel him in. I reach down to operate the pincers when I notice something strange on the radar. Something coming in fast—heading straight for us!

That can't be right? It looks like a—

BOOM!

The Freedom Ferry lurches backward. Luckily, my seatbelt keeps me from flying out of my chair, but as the ship rights itself my cheek slams down on the console.

That's gonna leave a mark.

I don't know what happened, but I can't worry about it now, I need to catch the Herald! But I can't spot him anywhere. Where'd he go?

Just then, the Freedom Ferry is lifted completely out of the water! I'm rising hundreds of feet into the air at ridiculous speed! And then, everything stops. I brace myself for a big fall, but nothing happens. Looking down, I see that, incredibly, the ship is balancing on a giant plume of water!

"You do not have clearance to fly over Japanese air space," comes a man's voice. "Identify yourself."

That's when I see a dude wearing red goggles and a blue wetsuit riding a wave like a surfboard. He makes a cutting motion with his arm, and my stomach drops as the Freedom Ferry free-falls toward the ocean! Then, with an upward sweep of his hand, I'm buoyed by another wave!

He was that blip on the radar!

He can control water!

"H-Hold on!" I yell, feeling queasy. "I'm Epic Zero! Who are you?"

"I am Tsunami," he says. "And you have five seconds to tell me whose government you work for, otherwise I will drown you in my sea." He lifts both hands, and I go flying back in the air.

"Wait!" I scream. "It's not what you think!"

I land with a thud on top of another wave! I'm totally seasick!

"Speak," he says. "Quickly."

"Look, I'm sorry if I broke some sort of international treaty, but I'm a member of the Freedom Force, and I'm trying to stop that fire guy before he escapes Earth and brings back something so big and nasty it'll knock your flippers off."

"What fire guy?" Tsunami asks.

Suddenly, a bright, orange streak breaks through the surface of the water and launches into the sky, leaving a blazing trail behind him.

"That fire guy," I say, watching the Herald disappear into the stratosphere. He got away. I had him and he got away. "Well, I guess we're all belly up now."

"You are a member of the Freedom Force?" Tsunami asks.

"Yeah," I say.

"But you are just a boy?"

"Yep," I say. "Can't deny that one."

"You are coming with us," Tsunami says.

"Us?" I say. "Who's 'us?'"

"*We* are the greatest heroes of the East," comes a booming voice to my left. "*We* are the Rising Suns."

I turn to find four other costumed characters hovering next to the Freedom Flyer. Where'd they come from? There's a big guy with a green cape and a dragon emblem on his chest, another guy dressed like a samurai warrior holding a glowing sword, a long-haired woman in a karate uniform, and a girl wearing a white mask, with a teardrop painted below her right eye.

Well, this doesn't look good.

Now that the Herald's gone, there's no reason for me to stick around. These guys are clearly Metas, and I suspect if I don't make a quick exit, I'll be in major trouble. The problem is, my wing is still on fire.

"Zen," Tsunami says. "Neutralize him."

What? But before I can react, I feel something enter my mind. And then, I hear a gentle voice.

Sleep.

The masked girl is a psychic!

Suddenly, my eyes feel droopy.

I need to use my powers!

I...

need...

to...

get...

out...

Meta Profile

Name: The Herald
Role: Cosmic Entity   Status: Active

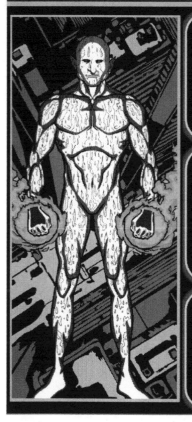

VITALS:

Race: Unknown
Real Name: Unknown
Height: 6'7"
Weight: 325 lbs
Eye Color: Yellow
Hair Color: Bald

META POWERS:

Class: Inapplicable
Power Level: Incalculable

- A being of extreme power that can generate and manipulate solar power
- Scouts and marks planets for Ravager to consume

CHARACTERISTICS:

Combat	100	
Durability	100	
Leadership	75	
Strategy	86	
Willpower	100	

FOUR

I GET TAKEN HOSTAGE

"Wake up!"

The girl's voice rings in my brain. My eyes jolt open, then close quickly from the bright spotlight glaring in my face. Squinting, I take in my surroundings.

I'm sitting at a table in a small room. Across the way are five figures shrouded in darkness. But I don't need to see them to know who they are.

I try standing up, but I can't move. I feel cold metal scrape against my wrists. Shackles?

Great. I'm trapped.

The figure seated across from me shifts in his chair, his muscled silhouette growing larger as he leans forward. I'm pretty sure he's the big one, the one with the dragon insignia on his chest. "Who was the red, flying man?" he demands.

"Santa Claus," I answer hoarsely. My throat is dry, like I haven't had water in days. How long have I been here?

"I will ask you again," he says, more sternly this time. "Who was the man of fire?"

I stare at my inquisitor—his face still hidden in shadows. I could lie, but at this point I've got nothing to lose. I'm clearly not talking my way out of this one.

"He's called the Herald," I say. "He's a scout for the cosmic monstrosity called Ravager, the Annihilator of Worlds. I had him captured, but thanks to your fishy friend over there, he got away. Now he'll come back with that planet-eating terror and destroy us all."

My captors exchange words in Japanese. Unfortunately, I'm not very multi-lingual. I barely remember a handful of middle-grade Spanish, like 'me aprietan mucho los zapatos.' So, I can't understand a darn thing they're saying.

"How did you come to our land?" the man continues.

"Um, by jet," I say. Why are they asking me that? I mean, I was in the Freedom Ferry when they captured me.

There's more back and forth in Japanese.

The man turns back and faces me. "Let me rephrase my question to be more precise. This jet, from which planet does it originate?"

What? Which planet? Is this a trick question? I look at him like he's got two heads and say, "Um, Earth."

"Really?" he says. "Then how do you explain this?" He looks back at his armored colleague and calls, "Silent Samurai."

Suddenly, the guy dressed in samurai gear steps forward and draws his sword. It's long and sharp and could probably slice me into a million pieces. Then, he raises it over his head!

"Whoa, big fella!" I say. "Watch where you're pointing that thing!"

But when he swings downward, the sword misses me and produces some kind of energy field in its wake. Then, the vibrating energy forms into a holographic image. That looks like me! And the Rising Suns! Wait a minute, it's a re-creation of our fight!

There's the Freedom Ferry—with me inside! I watch Zen wave her arm, putting me to sleep. And then, the Silent Samurai guy and the karate woman board the Freedom Ferry and pull my unconscious body out.

Watching myself get captured is weird. But then, things get weirder.

Suddenly, the Freedom Flyer goes transparent! And then it comes back again! It does this several times like it's popping in and out of the scene. And then, to my astonishment, it's gone! Like, completely vanished!

What's happening? I mean, I could have been inside that thing!

"Now," the man continues. "Where did you send your ship? Back to your planet?"

"What?" I say. "No, I-I don't know what happened."

"Not true!" he bellows, slamming his fist onto the table which promptly splits in two. "Do I need to be more persuasive?"

"Stop, Green Dragon," the karate-clad woman says. "Look at his eyes. It is clear the child does not know."

"I will judge what the child does and does not know, Fight Master," the Green Dragon says. "Look me in the eyes, boy."

Suddenly, they kill the spotlight and I can see everyone clearly. Behind the Green Dragon stand the rest of the Rising Suns. Fight Master must be the woman. And there's Zen, and Tsunami, and Silent Samurai.

"Look," I say. "This is all a big misunderstanding. I'm not from another planet, I'm a superhero from America. I was simply trying to save the planet from extermination, that's all. Maybe if you call the Freedom Force we can straighten this whole thing out and I can go home?"

"You are going nowhere," Green Dragon says. "Perhaps you are a spy, capturing unlawful surveillance of our country. Did you transport your findings back to your government in that ship?"

"No, I'm just a kid."

"Then listen closely, kid," Green Dragon says. "Only when you return the jet can we begin to discuss the remote possibility of your freedom."

"But I didn't make it disappear."

"Perhaps an evening in solitary confinement will help revive your memory," he says.

"Now hang on—"

"Zen."

Oh no.

"Sleep," she says, inside my head.

And I'm out.

***

When I wake up, it takes about a nanosecond to realize I'm in serious trouble. I'm a prisoner inside the tiniest cell in existence. But what it lacks in square footage it more than makes up for in efficiency, because there's only me, a cot, and a toilet. Yep, that's pretty much everything you need in life.

I run my hand along the surface of the wall. It's tungsten steel, the strongest metal on Earth. There's no way I'm getting out of here. Even the door looks triple-reinforced.

I feel super groggy, so I try shaking out the cobwebs. That Zen girl may be a more dangerous psychic than Mom. I mean, I never even felt her enter my mind. The next time I see her, I'm going on the offensive.

I stand up and stretch my legs. There's not much room to walk around. And because there's no window, I can't tell if it's day or night.

How did I get myself into this mess? I'm sure my parents found my note and are flipping out by now. If I could just get in contact with them they'd bust me out of here. Then we'd show the Rising Suns what real good guys look like.

My mind drifts to Ravager. While I'm rotting in this cell, the Herald is probably leading that monster straight to Earth by now. The only way to stop him is with the Orb of Oblivion, but that's gone. And who knows if it would have worked anyway? Especially in my hands.

I've got to get out of here! I push hard against the door, not that I expect anything to happen. I'm absolutely kicking myself for leaving my utility belt on the Waystation. Not that it would have mattered because I'm guessing the Rising Suns would have taken it from me anyway.

I'm about to pound on the wall and yell for help when I lose my balance. I guess I'm not as steady as I thought. And my vision is still sort of blurry.

Wait a minute?

Blurry!

The Freedom Ferry was blurry!

It was out of focus—fading in and out before it disappeared. What did the Herald say about the Blur? Something about whole galaxies collapsing, vanishing in the blink of an eye.

O.M.G.

Was the Freedom Ferry a sign? Is our galaxy next to disappear?

I feel myself hyperventilating. I've got to get out of here! I've got to tell the Freedom Force! Maybe TechnocRat will know what to do!

But I'm trapped. And soon, the Rising Suns are going to come back for me, and who knows what they'll do when I don't tell them what they want to hear. If I only had the power to get out of this joint. To bust out like Dad. Or teleport like Makeshift. Or jump into a wormhole like... like...

Wind Walker!

That's it!

The last time I saw him, he transported me home from another universe. What did he say before he took off? Call him if I ever needed help? But he didn't give me a communications device or anything. And how's he going to find me here? I don't even know where I am.

I close my eyes.

Wind Walker! I call out with my mind.

Then, I open my eyes and wait, but there's nothing.

Okay, that's not going to work.

I put my ear to the door—there's no noise on the other side. I scan the room for security cameras or monitoring equipment. Nothing. Well, what have I got to lose? Here goes nothing.

I take a deep breath, and yell as loud as I can, "WIND WALKER!"

Suddenly, a blue-skinned man with long, dark hair materializes before my eyes.

It's him! He's here!

But something is wrong. He's holding his right arm, and there's a large slash across his face. And his eyes. They look... defeated?

"Epic Zero," Wind Walker says feebly. "I came as soon as I heard your call. I am sorry for the delay."

"There wasn't any delay. What happened to you? What's wrong?"

"I-I will be fine, my friend," he replies. "But soon, my world—all of our worlds, will not be."

"Does this have to do with the Blur?" I ask.

"The Blur?" he says surprised. "Then you are aware of the great cosmic upheaval. Yes, I suppose we could call it that. For at this very moment, the multiverse is collapsing—blurring into one. And when it is complete, every mirror universe except for one will be destroyed, taking countless lives with it."

"What can we do?" I ask. "There's got to be a way to stop it?"

Wind Walker brushes a strand of hair off his face and looks me straight in the eyes. "I do not know," he says. "My powers only allow me to walk across dimensions. I have tried to intervene in every way possible. But all I can do is watch helplessly as whole universes die."

"The Herald said this is happening because Order

and Chaos were destroyed," I say.

"The Herald was here?" Wind Walker says, his eyes widening.

"Yes, and now Ravager is loose—coming here to destroy my planet."

Wind Walker looks at me solemnly. "I am sorry, my friend. I am afraid there is nothing we can do."

"Nothing?" I shout. "I won't accept nothing. Look, I don't know how to stop this 'Blur thing' either. But, I'm not going to sit around and watch Ravager eat my home."

"Of course," Wind Walker says. "I am sorry. You are right. We are heroes and need to act as such. Even in the face of impossible odds. Let me assist you. I assume you contacted me to free you from this prison?"

That's a good start. But then I've got to figure out a way to destroy Ravager. And the only way to do that is with the Orb of Oblivion.

But my Orb is gone.

My Orb.

The words strike me funny. I mean, the Orb was never mine. It chose me. I never chose it.

My Orb.

And then a lightbulb goes off. Wait a minute. Wind Walker can cross universes, which means…

He can take me to another universe!

A mirror universe!

Where there might be a mirror Orb of Oblivion!

"Big guy," I say. "I know exactly what I need you to

do."

Just then, we hear angry voices outside.

The Rising Suns!

I leap into Wind Walker's arms and shout, "Get us out of here!"

"Who is that?" Wind Walker asks.

"Later!" I yell. "Right now, I need less talking, more worm-holing!"

Suddenly, the door swings open and Green Dragon bursts in.

But he's too late.

Because we're gone!

Meta Profile
The Rising Suns

Green Dragon

Class: Super Strength
Meta: ▩▩▩▩▢

Fight Master

Class: Meta-Morph
Meta: ▩▩▩▩▢

Zen

Class: Psychic
Meta: ▩▩▩▢

Tsunami

Class: Energy Manipulator
Meta: ▩▩▩▩▢

Silent Samurai

Class: Magic
Meta: ▩▩▩▩▢

FIVE

I GO WHERE NO KID HAS GONE BEFORE

We hit the ground hard.

Wind Walker touches down smoothly, but I'm wobblier than a newborn deer. Everything is spinning like crazy, so I reach out for something—anything—to keep from toppling over. Then, I feel Wind Walker grab my arms, steadying me.

"Are you okay?" he asks.

Wow! I completely forgot what a roller coaster ride it is traveling through Wind Walker's inter-dimensional wormholes. "I-I think so," I say. "You know, I'm not sure I meet the height requirements to ride that thing."

After a few seconds, I get my bearings, but something is off. I mean, why are birds the only things at eye level?

That's when I realize we're up high, standing on top of some green structure with giant spikes flaring out in all directions. I clutch Wind Walker's arm and peer over the edge. There's like, all these tiny people milling around below.

Hang on, those aren't tiny people—they're real-sized people! Which means we must be hundreds of feet in the air!

I look back at Wind Walker and see a gigantic hand holding a torch behind him.

No way!

"We're on top of the freaking Statue of Liberty!"

"Yes," Wind Walker says. "You desired freedom. This is the first place that came to mind."

"Strangely," I say, "that kind of makes sense."

"Shall I take you home now?"

Home? Now there's a great question.

Honestly, going home never crossed my mind. While it would be great to have the Freedom Force by my side, there's so many of them it would ruin any possibility of surprise. Besides, if I told them what I was planning to do they would try to stop me. So, that pretty much seals the deal.

No home. No family.

I'm going solo.

"No thanks," I say. "But, I need you to drop me somewhere else. And you've got to promise not to tell anybody. Deal?"

Wind Walker gives me a suspicious look. "Deal."

***

Okay, I'm clearly nuts for doing this again.

Wind Walker's got me by the arm, dragging me through yet another wormhole of doom. It's like we're swimming inside a pitch-black washing machine. I feel the space narrowing around us, closing in, while an unrelenting wind blows against our faces.

I'm wiped. This is the longest wormhole I've ever been through. It feels like we've been traveling forever. Then, without warning, we POP out the other side. Wind Walker lands with the grace of a cat. I hit the ground like a hippopotamus.

"Are you hurt?" Wind Walker asks.

"Just my pride," I mutter, lying face down. "Don't worry, I'll be fine."

"Are you certain about this?" he asks.

I scramble to my feet, my stomach still doing flips. Wind Walker studies my face for signs of weakness, but I'm not breaking. No matter how terrified I am—and believe me, I'm terrified—I've got a job to do.

"Very well," he says. "Remember, you are no longer on your world. Places may appear identical, people may look familiar, but nothing is as it seems. For as long as you remain here, your greatest enemy is yourself. If you lower your guard, even for a second, it could cost you your life."

I take a deep breath and force a smile. "Okay, okay," I say. "I've got it. I can handle this."

"I hope so," Wind Walker says. "Now, I must try to solve the riddle of the Blur before it is too late. Good luck, Epic Zero. If you need me, call my name. Hopefully, I will be able to return for you."

"Good luck," I say, as we shake hands.

"Do not forget what I told you," he says. Then, he steps into a black void and disappears.

I'm alone.

In Keystone City.

On another Earth.

Earth 2.

When I battled on Arena World, I learned that I lived on just one version of Earth. That my reality was only one version of reality and there were possibly billions of other realities out there. Wind Walker called them mirror universes. So, while I exist in my world, other versions of me likely exist in other worlds.

At first, it was hard to get my head around that idea—until I met Grace 2 and Mom 2. Then, I realized it was real. There really are mirror universes out there.

And while I may not have the Orb of Oblivion to stop Ravager from destroying my world, I'm pretty sure there's one person in this world who has another Orb of Oblivion.

Elliott 2.

From what Grace 2 told me about him, he's not like me at all. He's evil and supposedly rules his Earth with an iron fist. Plus, he's blond while my hair is brown which is kind of strange to imagine.

So, my three-part plan is simple. First, get to Earth 2. Check—thanks to Wind Walker's dimension-crossing ability. Second, find Elliott 2 and steal the second Orb of Oblivion. Third, get back to my world in time to prevent Ravager from destroying it.

It seems simple enough. Right?

Wrong, and I know it, but I can't look back now. Not if I have a shot at saving my Earth.

So, where would I be hanging out if I were an evil version of myself?

Suddenly, I hear the unmistakable rumbling of an oncoming car, so I dive behind the nearest hedge. Peeking through the shrubbery, I watch as a camouflaged jeep drives past carrying three costumed goons. That's weird, those guys looked like the Terror Triplets, a trio of Meta 1 villains on my world. What are they doing casually driving around a nice suburban neighborhood?

But as I look around from my hiding spot, I realize the neighborhood isn't nearly as nice as I thought it was. Every house looks abandoned and in need of massive repairs. Windows are smashed. Front doors are kicked in. Roofs have gaping holes. It's like a war was waged here, and no one bothered cleaning up the mess!

Then, I remember my talks with Grace 2 on Arena World. She told me that with all of the heroes out of the picture, criminal Meta gangs had taken over everything and battled over turf. At the time, I thought that sounded bad, but I never imagined it would be this bad. I mean, there aren't any regular people around. And where did all the heroes go?

This is completely depressing. And to top it off, I have no idea what to do next. But one thing I do know is that I can't sit here.

I wait for the jeep to speed past, and then race across the street as fast as I can. Ducking behind a tree, I catch a street sign dangling loosely from its pole. Wait a minute! I'm on High Street. So, that means I'm only a few blocks away from...

The Prop House!

Suddenly, things are looking up! In my world, the Prop House was the fake house we used to travel from the Waystation to Earth and back again. If it's the same thing here, then maybe I can use the Transporter to find Grace 2 and the Freedom Force and pull this thing off!

I feel strangely giddy booking down the street towards my old home. I reach the end of the road and hang a left. Just a few more blocks to go. This is going to be so much easier than I thought!

Then, I hear footsteps behind me.

Somebody is running after me.

Closing in on me.

I spin around, ready for a fight, but to my surprise, there's no one there. That's weird, I could have sworn I heard something. I shake my head. I mean, it wouldn't be the first time my mind has played tricks on me.

Suddenly, out of the corner of my eye, I catch movement from high above. I throw myself beneath a burnt-out truck and look up. Six Metas are soaring high up above. I can't tell who they are, but it looks like they're flying in a 'V' formation—like they're on patrol!

I scoot as far beneath the truck as I can, my heart pounding a mile a minute. Hopefully, they didn't see me. But how could they miss me? I was running down the middle of the street like a bonehead! If I get captured before I can even get inside the Prop House, it's over.

I wait a few minutes before I risk poking my head out. When I finally do, the patrol is gone. And even better, I spot the Prop House straight ahead. Seeing it again takes my breath away, but not for the reasons I'd hoped.

The house is leaning hard to the left. The roof is sagging, the door and windows are boarded up, and the posts flanking the front porch are piles of rubble scattered over the patch-work front lawn.

It's a teardown.

All the air escapes from my happiness balloon.

There's not going to be any reunion with Grace 2 and the Freedom Force. I'm on my own.

Seeing the Prop House like this is utterly

heartbreaking. I think of all the good times we had there. Like when Grace and I hid TechnocRat's electromagnetic power rods and accidentally shorted out the Waystation. Or when we tracked Dog-Gone's gravy-stained footprints here after he stole the Thanksgiving turkey. Or when our neighbor called the cops when Dad forgot to take off his mask before mowing the lawn.

Of course, there was also plenty of drama. Like the countless times I took the Transporter to school while Grace was off fighting with the Freedom Force. Or when the Worm's goons broke in and discovered the Waystation. After that, we removed the Transporter and sold the Prop House, but I miss it. Strangely, it was the only 'normal' home I ever had.

Even though it's hopeless, I'm still itching to look inside. I'm sure the Transporter is long gone, but I'm curious to see if anything else was left behind. I mean, we decorated the Prop House with family pictures and other sentimental stuff. Maybe there's some clue in there I can use to track down Grace 2.

I make sure I'm in the clear, and then break for it. Stepping onto the Prop House's dilapidated porch, I press my ear against the boarded door. Just as I thought, there's no noise coming from inside. So, I push hard against the wood, opening a space just large enough to slip inside.

It's dark.

Instinctively, I reach for the light switch and flick it

on. Surprisingly, it works!

And then I get the shock of my life.

The blue sofas, the coffee table, the TV, the pictures. They're all here. In perfect condition.

But… how can that be?

I walk through the room stunned. It's an exact replica of the Prop House on my world. Then, I remember…

The full-length mirror! The miniature Statue of Liberty! They're here!

Is it possible?

I walk over and wrap my hand around the mini figurine when…

"Let go," commands a deep, voice.

What the—?

I turn to find the silhouette of a large, broad-shouldered man filling the doorframe. A dead rabbit swings freely by its ears in his left hand.

I'm not sure what to do. There's nowhere to run. And if I pull the Statue of Liberty, there may not be a Transporter to escape into.

I'm trapped.

Then, he steps into the light. He looks like a mountain man—with dark, scraggly hair and a bushy mustache and beard. He's wearing a long trench coat that covers his body from his shoulders to his legs.

There's something oddly familiar about him.

Then, I notice his blue eyes staring me down.

And that's when I realize I know him.

O! M! G!

"D-Dad?" I stammer.

"I don't know why you came back, Elliott," he says. "But I'll tell you this, one of us isn't leaving here alive!"

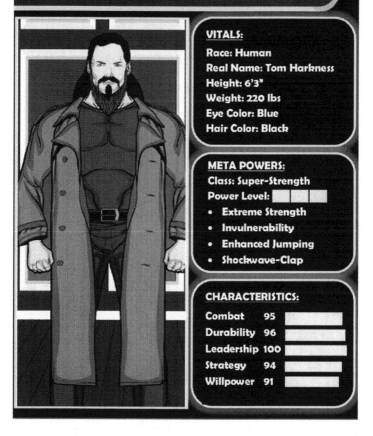

Meta Profile

Name: Captain Justice 2
Role: Hero   Status: Inactive

VITALS:

Race: Human
Real Name: Tom Harkness
Height: 6'3"
Weight: 220 lbs
Eye Color: Blue
Hair Color: Black

META POWERS:

Class: Super-Strength
Power Level: ▮▮▮▮
- Extreme Strength
- Invulnerability
- Enhanced Jumping
- Shockwave-Clap

CHARACTERISTICS:

Combat	95
Durability	96
Leadership	100
Strategy	94
Willpower	91

SIX

I LEARN TO TRUST NO ONE

Dad 2 is about to ground me, but I mean like, bury me six feet under.

"Sorry, son," he says, tossing the dead rabbit to the floor. "But you've had this coming for a long, long time."

I watch his giant muscles ripple as he removes his trench coat. He thinks I'm his kid, the evil ruler of his world! Somehow, I've got to convince him I'm not. Otherwise, I'll be worse off than that rabbit!

"Listen, Dad—I mean, Captain Justice, I know this will be surprising to hear, but I'm not your son." I've got to think fast. I could wipe his powers, but he'd easily crush me anyway. Plus, that would only convince him I'm exactly who he thinks I am. I need a different approach. Pronto!

"No more games, Elliott," he says, wiping his long, dark hair out of his face. "I'm tired of your games."

That's it! Hair!

"Wait!" I say, pointing to my head. "Look! I've got dark hair, just like you."

"So?" he says. "It won't stop me from doing what I need to do."

"No," I say. "Don't you get it? *Your* son has blond hair. I'm not who you think I am. I'm Elliott but from a different universe."

This isn't working! He's still coming at me! I need another approach!

"I'm friends with your daughter, Grace. And I saved your wife's life."

That part stops him cold. I keep going. "The last time I saw her she was a villain. But then I saved her from death and she promised to become a hero again."

"She promised what?" he says. "Who are you?"

"I'm a hero from a mirror universe. I'm here to stop your son, just like you! So please don't clobber me!"

Dad 2 looks at me, confused. "A mirror universe? TechnocRat talked about it once, but I never thought it was possible."

"Oh, it's possible," I say. "In fact, it's real. Your world is exactly like mine, but all mixed up. In my world, I'm a hero—a member of the Freedom Force—just like you."

Suddenly, his face falls. "I'm no hero. Not anymore."

Then, I remember what Grace 2 told me. That her version of Dad gave up the superhero business after my double took over his planet, outlawed all superheroes, and turned his wife into a supervillain.

"So, you just hide in here?" I ask. "While all that bad stuff is happening outside?"

He strolls over to the sofa and sits down, his head in his hands. "What else can I do?"

"You can fight!" I say strongly. I can't believe my ears. Captain Justice 2 is a... coward?

"For what?" he says. "There are hundreds of Meta villains out there, all of whom would love to make a name for themselves by hauling me in. You think I want to get captured and have you—or my kid, rather—cancel my powers permanently and feed me to the wolves? They'll lock me up and make an example out of me. Just like they did to Master Mime and Blue Bolt."

Cancel his powers? What's he talking about?

"It's safer in here," he continues. "Thankfully, I managed to steal TechnocRat's Distorter before our headquarters was overrun. The Distorter makes the house look like a disaster on the outside, but inside it's fine. No one ever thinks to look in here. To survive, all I need to do is hunt for food and stay out of trouble."

Did he say headquarters? If I can get to the Freedom Force's headquarters, then I may be able to find Grace 2.

"You said your headquarters was overrun," I say. "Can you take me there? Can you take me to the

Waystation?"

"Waystation," he says. "What's a Waystation?"

"Hang on," I say shocked. "Do you mean there's no—" Suddenly, I notice the Statue of Liberty figurine is fading in and out!

"What are you doing?" he asks.

"Nothing," I say. Is that the Blur?

He stands up and races over to it. One second the mini statue is there, the next, it's gone. He reaches for it.

"Wait!" I warn. "Don't touch it. It's going to vanish. For good."

Then, as if on cue, it disappears.

"Bring it back!" he cries.

"Relax," I say. "It's just a statue. On my world, it took my whole Freedom Ferry."

"Get out of my way," he says, bumping me aside. His eyes look crazed, like something is seriously wrong. He leans over and lifts the mirror. It must weigh hundreds of pounds, but for him it's nothing.

"No!" he says, frantically looking inside the empty space behind the mirror. "It's gone!"

I peek inside. There's no Transporter. Great. Now I've got zero chance of finding Grace 2.

"The Distorter," he says. "I hid the Distorter in here, behind the mirror. And now it's gone!"

"Sorry about that," I say. "But look, I've got bigger problems. See, there's this cosmic alien mist coming to swallow my Earth, so I really need to find your son and get something from him. You wouldn't happen to know where to find him, would you?"

But he can't hear me. His face is flush with anger. "It's your fault the Distorter is gone! It's your fault I'm going to get caught! You're going to pay for this!"

I get the sense this is going downhill fast.

He turns, about to drop the mirror and grab me, when—out of nowhere—his trench coat comes flying across the room and drapes over his head.

"Hey!" he yells.

How did that happen?

Then, he's shoved back into the empty space behind the mirror. The giant mirror SLAMS down to the floor, trapping him inside. I don't know what's happening, but I know I've got seconds to get out of here before he busts through that mirror.

But before I can move, a German Shepherd appears before my eyes.

"Dog-Gone!"

His tail wags from side to side, and then he takes off, heading out of the Prop House through a large opening he made in the boarded door. I hear Dad 2 yelling something from behind the mirror, but I'm not sticking around to find out what.

I squeeze through the hole and bolt into the front yard. Dog-Gone is way ahead, and I'm huffing to keep up. I'll tell you one thing, humans may have opposable thumbs, but when it comes to running for your life I'd take four legs any day of the week.

I glance back at the Prop House, and to my surprise, it no longer looks like a dump. The cherry red door is back. As are the windows, posts, roof, and landscaping. Dad 2 was right, that Distorter really worked.

I try making sense of what just happened. I can't believe Dad 2 has given up. I mean, he's not my dad but he's still Captain Justice, the leader of the freaking Freedom Force! Suddenly, Wind Walker's words ring truer than ever: *nothing is as it seems.*

Dog-Gone races down the block and peels off between two abandoned houses. I'm probably a block behind him, so I dig deep and try to pick up speed. I don't know how he tracked me down, but boy I'm glad he did. Right now, a friendly face is exactly what I need.

I hit the spot where he turned off, but Dog-Gone is nowhere to be found.

"Dog-Gone?" I whisper. What happened to that mutt? Did he take off or did something bad happen to him? I look around for clues, like footprints, doggie doo—anything—when something plows into me, taking out my legs!

I land hard on my rear with a thud. But before I can react, I feel hot breath, accompanied by a low, threatening growl.

"Dog-Gone?" I say. "What are you doing?" Dog-Gone's head appears inches from my face and I'm staring at his razor-sharp teeth. Clearly, he's not so happy to see me.

"Whoa, boy," I say. "It's me, Elliott, your mas… ter."

And then it hits me. This isn't my Dog-Gone. It's Dog-Gone 2! And based on his incredible sense of smell, he knows I'm not his Elliott!

He growls again—a menacing, throaty growl.

"Hang on," I plead. "I never tricked you. You saved me, remember?"

Another growl.

"Look, we both know I'm not your Elliott. But that doesn't mean I'm a bad person. I'm just looking for your master. Do you know where he is?"

Suddenly, he lets out a high-pitched whimper.

What's going on? Why is he reacting that way? Hold on. I would never, *ever* let my Dog-Gone roam the streets alone unsupervised. He could get hurt. And this world is way more dangerous than mine.

So, maybe that means…

"Is your Elliott missing?"

Dog-Gone 2 bows his head and lets out another whimper.

He *is* missing!

"Look, boy," I say. "That's why I'm here. I'm trying to find your Elliott too. Maybe we can work together and figure out where he is? What do you say?"

The German Shepherd studies me with his big, brown eyes. I try to look trustworthy. After all, I'm not going to tell him I'm only here to steal the Orb of Oblivion.

I feel wet slobber on my chin.

I guess that's a yes!

Dog-Gone 2 backs up and I get to my feet. "Okay, maybe we should start with where you saw him last."

The mutt nods and takes off again. Great, a dog that's even more impulsive than mine! I don't know where we're heading, but my thoughts are completely scattered.

I mean, what could have happened to Elliott 2?

Maybe somebody took him out? But if he has the Orb of Oblivion, then whoever did that must be pretty powerful.

Or maybe the Orb took over his mind? I know how powerful the Orb can be, and my greatest fear was always losing control. It's possible Elliott 2 lost the battle and the Orb is using him as its host.

The very thought makes me shudder.

I catch up with Dog-Gone 2 who's waiting for me behind a tall hedge. He's panting lightly, meanwhile, my lungs are burning. You'd think after all the times I've run from danger, I'd have more endurance by now.

"Is this where... you saw him last?" I wheeze.

Dog-Gone nods his head 'yes,' and walks to the other side. I round the corner and find him standing stock-still, staring straight ahead. As I see what he's pointing at, my stomach sinks and I realize this mission is going to be a lot harder than I imagined.

Because rising before us is a monstrous structure resembling a steel octopus.

Lockdown.

Meta Profile

Name: Dog-Gone 2
Role: Villain   Status: Active

VITALS:

Breed: German Shepherd
Real Name: Dog-Gone
Height: 2'1" (at shoulder)
Weight: 85 lbs
Eye Color: Dark Brown
Hair Color: Brown/Black

META POWERS:

Class: Meta-morph
Power Level:
- Considerable Invisibility
- Can turn all or part of body invisible

CHARACTERISTICS:

Combat	45	
Durability	16	
Leadership	10	
Strategy	12	
Willpower	56	

SEVEN

I CAN'T BELIEVE MY BAD LUCK

Well, this is the last place I thought I'd ever be.

On my Earth, Lockdown is the Meta-Maximum Federal Penitentiary designed to keep the world's most dangerous super-powered villains under lock and key. Essentially, it's where the good guys put away the bad guys—for good. So, to say I'm shocked by what I'm seeing is a gross understatement.

The inmates have taken over the asylum.

Lockdown looks like an ant farm for costumed criminals. They're manning guard towers, patrolling the walls—even guarding the front gates! There isn't a superhero or law enforcement officer in sight.

I glance over at Dog-Gone 2 who's busy relieving himself on a nearby tree. I had asked that fleabag to take me to the last place he saw Elliott 2, but I never thought it would be here. Maybe he misheard me?

I mean, if he's like my Dog-Gone, he has what I'd call 'selective hearing.' If you're miles away and open a bag of potato chips he's by your side in a flash, but if you ask him to get his snout out of the trash can it's like his ears are suddenly stuffed with cotton. Go figure.

"Dog-Gone," I whisper. "Are you sure about this? Remember, I asked you to take me to where you saw your master last."

Dog-Gone nods and turns back to Lockdown.

Just. Freaking. Wonderful.

Not only do we need to break into an impenetrable prison controlled by super-powered villains, but we also need to get Elliott 2 out before we're caught, killed, or all of the above. Sounds like a suicide run.

"We need a plan," I say, looking to the heavens for inspiration. "And since I've got the bigger brain, I guess it's up to me. Let's figure this out. We need to get inside without being seen, which should be easy for you. Unfortunately, we just can't march up to the front gates and—"

I hear a rustling noise. The next thing I know, Dog-Gone 2 is wading through the underbrush heading straight for Lockdown's front gates! And he's not invisible!

I duck behind the hedges. "Dog-Gone!" I whisper firmly. "Dog-Gone, come! Get back here! Bad dog!"

But it's too late, he's halfway to the gates by now. I hear shouting when the watchtower guards finally see him. That's fine, he can get caught if he wants to, but not me. No siree Bob! I'm getting out of here while I still c—

Wait a minute! What's he doing? Why is he turning around and facing me? He's just standing there, using his nose like a pointer.

That mongrel! He's selling me out! I've got to split!

But it's too late.

The Super-Speedsters reach me first. I recognize them from their Meta-profiles: Speed Demon, Whirlwind, Break-Neck. Then, the Flyers drop in: Atmo-Spear, Dark Storm, Bicyclone, Terrible Tempest. Then come all the rest—waves of them.

I'm surrounded.

"Hey, it's great to see you guys," I say. "How's the family?"

Just then, a pack of villains split apart, and a masked figure wearing a long, dark robe approaches. He looks me up and down through the white slits in his black mask. "Your Excellency," he says, with a grisly voice. Then, he bends in a slight bow. "We are thankful for your safe return."

Your Excellency? Is he talking to me?

Wait a minute! That voice. I know that voice!

"Shadow Hawk? What are you doing at Lockdown?"

"Of course, your Excellency," he says, looking surprised. "Where else would I be? I see Dog-Gone found you. Fortunately, that saves us from paying a large bounty, although now I'm sure I need to find a lifetime supply of dog biscuits. So, where did you wander off to? And if you don't mind me asking, what happened to your hair?"

My hair? I reach up and touch my head. Wait a minute, my hair! They think I'm Elliott 2—the ruler of this world! So, that means Shadow Hawk 2 must be evil too. This is so weird, but I've got to play along!

"I went for a stroll," I say.

"Three weeks is quite a long stroll, your Excellency," Shadow Hawk 2 says, his eyes narrowing. "And your hair?"

Okay, think fast. I need an excuse for why I'm not blond. "Oh, I ran into some weird Meta 1 hero named Color Clash. He turned my hair brown, so I made sure he saw black and blue."

"I see," he says, looking at the villains around us. "Perhaps we should discuss this at a more appropriate time. Why don't we head back to Lockdown? You seem tired and I'm sure you're hungry. Besides, in your absence we found something I'm sure will pique your interest. Shall we?"

I nod, and he leads us towards the prison. The villains fall in line, as does Dog-Gone 2 who pads next to me with his head held high.

"Okay," I whisper. "Maybe you have the bigger brain. But next time, warn me first."

Dog-Gone 2 lets out an "I-told-you-so" growl as we march straight through the front gates. I peer up at the main building and think back to the last time I was here—with K'ami.

This is where the Worm brainwashed and freed an army of Meta 3 prisoners. This is where we fought the Blood Bringers over the Orb of Oblivion. This is where K'ami died.

It's strange how often I dream about that day, but no matter how many times I relive it, it always ends in the same nightmare—with me holding K'ami's lifeless body. K'ami sacrificed her life for me—for all of us. I wonder if I could ever do the same?

As we enter the main building, I hear her voice, calmly saying: *Never show weakness.*

And she's right. On the outside, I keep a poker face, but inside I'm a mess. I mean, I'm being escorted inside a flipping prison by a bunch of Meta prisoners! This wasn't exactly the plan I had in mind. But it's not like I've got better options.

We walk through several dimly lit hallways until we reach a security checkpoint. Shadow Hawk 2 swipes a card and the doors open into another hallway lined with dozens of cell doors. A sign above reads: *Former Hero Wing 5: Official Access Only.*

Former Hero wing? What does that mean?

Shadow Hawk 2 continues down the hall. As we pass by each cell, I read the signs:

Cell#27: Magnet Man — ex-Meta 2: Former member of the Hero Hive. Used to control magnetic objects. Is permitted to use silverware at mealtimes.

Cell#28: Electric Defender — ex-Meta 3: Former member of the Strike Force. Once able to fire electricity from his body. Is permitted to shower daily.

Cell#29: Blue Bolt — ex-Meta 3: Former member of the Freedom Force. Once able to move at super speed. Is allowed outdoor exercise once per day.

Blue Bolt? Or rather, Blue Bolt 2?

I stop and look inside the window. Blue Bolt is sitting cross-legged on the floor, her head hung low. She looks weak—almost broken.

Suddenly, Shadow Hawk 2 is by my side. "Pathetic, isn't she?"

Anger wells up inside me, but I can't blow my cover.

"She's powerless?" I ask.

"Completely," Shadow Hawk 2 says. "You saw to that, remember?"

Me? That's right! Back on Arena World, Grace 2 told me my evil double used his powers to render heroes powerless. Now what Captain Justice 2 said about having his powers canceled makes perfect sense! I can't look surprised.

"Of course," I say. "Um, I forgot. How long has she been in there again?"

"I don't know," he says. "Three months, maybe four. But don't worry, we're not feeding her much. We're only keeping her around until her friends inevitably try to rescue her. Once we capture them, we'll dispose of her like all the rest. Thank goodness heroes are so predictable."

"Y-You mean you're using her as... bait?"

"Yes, of course," he says, throwing me a suspicious look. "Those were your orders."

"Right," I say quickly. "Sorry, it's been a long week."

"Three weeks," Shadow Hawk 2 reminds me. "But your strategy has been very effective. Since you went on your little stroll, we've captured every member of the Do-Gooders, the Great Samaritans, the Honor Roll, and sixteen out of twenty members of the Liberty Legion."

I know those teams! In my world, they're all superhero teams. Mostly Meta 1's and 2's, but still, they're good guys. This is completely nuts!

"But we're still working on the grand prize," he continues. "Come, I have more to show you."

I take one last look at Blue Bolt 2. This is worse than I thought. But even I have to admit it's a brilliant strategy. I mean, no respectable hero could sit back and watch their colleagues suffer like this.

Unless, of course, you're Captain Justice 2.

We pass the cells of other fallen heroes. But right before the exit, something catches my eye. There's a flash of movement, and then a face presses against the glass window.

Yellow eyes follow me as I move down the hallway. I

swear I've seen those eyes before. But where?

And then it hits me—Alligazer!

I flinch, fearing I'll be turned to stone. But then I realize if he's in here, he's powerless!

We reach the final set of double doors and I get an incredible sense of déjà vu. The last time I walked through here, I fought the battle to end all battles. Who knows what's waiting for me this time?

Shadow Hawk 2 swipes again, and the doors open.

A familiar courtyard stretches out before us. It's massive in size and open to the night sky. This time, there are rows and rows of chairs set out, all facing a giant, golden chair situated on a platform.

Shadow Hawk 2 steps to the side and motions. "Your throne, your Excellency."

My throne? Well, okay then. I smile and make my way over to the platform.

Just then, doors open on all sides of the courtyard, and hundreds of costumed creeps come spilling out. I've never seen so many bad guys in one place before. They line up in front of the chairs, their right hands across their hearts.

Um, okay. What's going on?

Shadow Hawk 2 approaches quickly and whispers in my ear. "Your Excellency, they will not sit until you do."

"Oh, yes, of course," I say. Then, I step up onto the platform and sit in the chair.

The villains follow suit.

Dog-Gone lies in front of me, forming a furry barrier between me and the crooks.

Hundreds of evil eyes are fixed on me. I feel really, really uncomfortable. I mean, what am I supposed to do now?

The next thing I know, Shadow Hawk 2 appears by my side and starts speaking. "My vile friends, thank you for putting aside your differences to join us for a most historic occasion. I am aware that many, if not all of you have attempted to further your positions during the temporary absence of our liege. But, as you can see, he has returned and is stronger than ever."

I sit up and try to look dangerous.

"Now," Shadow Hawk 2 continues. "Let's waste no more time. Let's get to the main event, the reason you are all gathered here today."

The criminals start buzzing. Something big is about to happen.

"Henchman!" Shadow Hawk 2 calls. "Bring forth the cage!"

Suddenly, a door opens and two strongmen enter the courtyard carrying a large, square-shaped object covered by a cloth. All eyes are on it as they place it in front of the platform.

"Watch and be warned!" Shadow Hawk 2 says. "For if you fail to comply with the commands of our King, what happens next may happen to you!"

Um, okay.

"Now," Shadow Hawk 2 says. "Bear witness to the superiority of our King as he renders another Meta hero powerless!"

Wait! What?

"Unveil the captive!"

Everyone rises as the cover is ripped off the box and my jaw drops in surprise.

"Now, Your Excellency," Shadow Hawk 2 shouts. "Destroy the girl!"

The villains erupt in a deafening cheer.

But to my horror, trapped inside the metal cage is a frightened, brown-haired girl wearing a blue costume with white stars.

It's Grace 2!

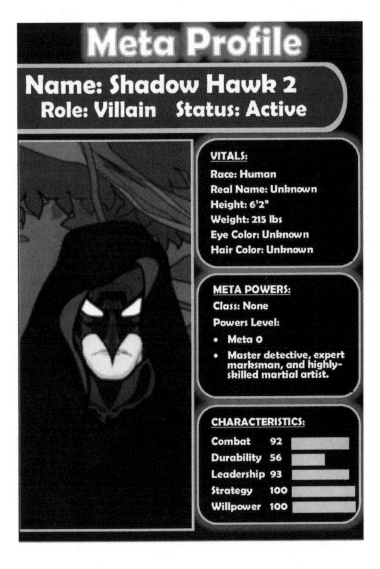

Meta Profile

Name: Shadow Hawk 2
Role: Villain   Status: Active

VITALS:

Race: Human
Real Name: Unknown
Height: 6'2"
Weight: 215 lbs
Eye Color: Unknown
Hair Color: Unknown

META POWERS:

Class: None

Powers Level:

- Meta 0
- Master detective, expert marksman, and highly-skilled martial artist.

CHARACTERISTICS:

Combat	92	
Durability	56	
Leadership	93	
Strategy	100	
Willpower	100	

EIGHT

I BECOME KING FOR A DAY

I think this is called 'irony.'

I mean, I've been looking for Grace 2 everywhere, and now, she's delivered to me on a silver platter! Of course, she's locked in a cage surrounded by hundreds of Meta villains who are cheering me on to remove her powers. So, it's not exactly the warm and fuzzy reunion I was hoping for.

"Zero her out!" comes a cry from the crowd.

"Filet that Flyer!" comes another.

Grace 2 looks at me, her blue eyes wide with fear.

Somehow, I've got to let her know I'm me, and not her brother, without giving myself away. Then, I've got to figure out how to get us out of this mess. Otherwise, they'll lock me up with her. Or worse.

"Your Excellency?" Shadow Hawk 2 says, the urgency in his voice signaling me to get on with it.

"Right," I say. I guess it's showtime.

As soon as I stand up, the villains go silent. I look at them, sitting at full attention like schoolchildren, waiting to see what I'm going to do next.

Boy, I only wish I knew.

I feel totally awkward standing here.

"I hate you!" Grace 2 shouts, breaking the silence.

The villains boo.

"I'll teach her to show respect!" someone yells.

Okay, I'd better do something before this gets out of hand. Time to turn on the acting chops.

"I'm guessing you're not feeling so glorious now, are you *Glory Girl*," I say mockingly, ensuring I can be heard throughout the courtyard. "You may be a member of the Freedom Force, but soon you'll find freedom hard to come by."

The villains roar with approval.

Okay, not bad. Got to keep going.

"See, you live in my world," I continue, "and in my world, heroes are a distraction, and distractions must be dealt with."

There's another cheer and I feel a strange boost of confidence. Who knew I'd be so good at this evil monologue stuff? Just keep talking. Keep stalling.

"Take her powers!" someone cries.

"Take 'em for good!"

Oh, geez, that's what they're all here to see, isn't it?

Okay, think!

I know I can't remove her powers permanently, but I *can* take them away temporarily. That should fool them, at least for now. But before I do that, I need to clue her in as to who I really am. So, how am I going to do that?

Wait, did I just say clue? That's it! I can drop in some clues!

"Now is the time!" I shout. "Now, I will remove the powers of this… this… jelly doughnut-eating girl."

Shadow Hawk 2 shoots me a funny look.

Okay, I'm probably blowing my cover, but I need Grace 2 to be sure, so I press on. "This terrible fate will befall her despite… having brown hair whereas, she may have been blond if she were born elsewhere. In addition, this punishment will be meted out despite her heroic achievements on Arena World where—"

"What are you doing?" Shadow Hawk 2 whispers sharply. "Get on with it!"

I look into the crowd. The villains are getting restless.

Did she get it?

I glance down at Grace 2, who's staring back at me with her arms crossed and a giant smirk across her face.

I'm taking that as a yes.

Okay, time to finish the job.

Pointing down at her, I declare, "Glory Girl, you've been a thorn in my side since the day I was born! Now, you will suffer the agony of being a Zero—for the rest of your life!"

I concentrate and then wash my powers over her.

Now for the big finale—the proof.

"Release her!" I command.

The villains rise to their feet as the two henchmen rip the cage apart.

To her surprise, Grace 2 is free.

"If it's freedom you want," I offer, "then go ahead and fly away. If you can."

Grace 2 raises her arms to lift off, but she can't.

"My powers," she says. "They're… gone."

The villains erupt in a victorious cheer.

It worked! It's over. Thank the stars it's over.

"Kill her!" someone yells.

Or not.

"No!" I react. "She's valuable to us. With her as our captive, we can lure the remaining members of the Freedom Force—like Ms. Understood and Captain Justice—to their deaths. Now, take her to a cell. Make sure she's as… uncomfortable as possible."

Grace 2 looks back at me, eyebrows raised, as the henchmen grab her arms roughly and drag her back inside Lockdown. Hopefully, she'll forgive me. But I had to look convincing. Now, I've got all these bad guys to deal with.

"This demonstration is over," I command. "Go back to your territories. All of you."

"Bow before your liege!" Shadow Hawk 2 orders.

All this pageantry is wonderful, but I'm not planning to stick around for tea and biscuits. Instead, I whisper to Dog-Gone 2, "Get me out of here."

Dog-Gone 2 scratches behind his ear, and then hops off the podium. I follow him to a large door on the far side of the courtyard. It's different than all the others, made from steel and surrounded by cameras. Dog-Gone 2 presses his nose against a touch screen that scans his schnoz. As the door slides open, I try to make sense of what I'm seeing.

Instead of a dull, dreary prison, I'm looking into a brightly lit, marble-tiled foyer.

"Is this where your master lives?" I ask.

Dog-Gone 2 nods and we go inside, the door sliding shut behind us.

He leads me down a hallway and past several prison cells which have been converted into living spaces of various functions. There's a game room filled with arcade machines, a recreation room with trampoline floors, a snack room packed with candy boxes and soda machines, and a reading room loaded with comic books and bean bag chairs.

It's like walking through heaven.

I follow the mutt into a large room at the end of the hallway, where I'm stopped in my tracks. I can't believe it.

It's my bedroom!

Or rather, it's exactly like my bedroom back on the

Waystation. It has the same blue-and-white bedspread, the same Batman posters on the wall, the same desk, the same cabinets, the same everything! There's just one difference. His walls are covered in black marker scribblings.

But stepping inside, I realize they aren't scribbles at all—they're equations! Hundreds of them, all over. So, here's another mirror-universe difference between Elliott 2 and me: he's a math whiz and I'm allergic to algebra.

What's with all the formulas? It's obvious he was trying to solve for something, but what? The only thing I know is there's not a snowball's chance in Hades I'm gonna figure it out.

Then, something catches my eye. It's an illustration of a bunch of tiny, irregular circles packed tightly together around a much larger circle. The little circles form a barrier of sorts. It looks strangely familiar.

It looks like... an asteroid belt?

"Feeling better?"

I jump out of my skin.

Shadow Hawk 2 is standing in the doorway with his arms folded across his chest. He steps inside. "Nice performance out there. Despite whatever you were doing to spoil the occasion."

Uh-oh, I need to be careful here. Shadow Hawk is no dummy. He knows something is up.

"So," he says, "did you make it?"

Make it? Make what?

"After all, you didn't think I'd ignore the fact that one of our Freedom Flyers went missing? Or did you?"

Oh, geez! This is worse than I thought.

"Based on the maps decorating your walls, I assumed you took the Freedom Flyer to reach that planet you were so desperately searching for."

Planet? My eyes dart back to the asteroid belt and the circle inside of it.

O! M! G!

I know exactly where Elliott 2 went!

"Well?" he asks. "Anything you'd like to share?"

My heart is racing but I try to stay cool. "Not really." The longer I stay in Lockdown, the faster he's going to find out I'm a phony. I stretch into a fake yawn. "You mind if we pick this up later? I'm wiped."

"Certainly, your Excellency," he says with a bow. "Let's do that. When we regroup, I'd love to hear the story of how you returned to Earth... *without* the Freedom Flyer you departed in." And then, he leaves.

He knows! Time to make my exit. But first I need to collect something.

"Dog-Gone, take me to Glory Girl's cell."

He looks at me funny and then cocks an ear.

I guess some things never change, even in a mirror universe. "Fine, I'll give you five doggie treats. Now do it!"

Dog-Gone takes off like a rocket. I chase him outside, back through the courtyard, and into the prison wing Grace 2 was dragged through. I get plenty of odd stares along the way, but I just smile, point to Dog-Gone, and say, "He loves a brisk walk."

He leads me into a small corridor that's empty save one prison cell and two large goons guarding it. I notice there's no window in the cell door which is good news for what I'm planning. So, here goes nothing.

"Open the door," I command.

The goons bow, and then swing the door open. Dog-Gone 2 and I step inside, and I instruct them to close it behind us, shutting us in.

The cell is dark and cramped. Slivers of daylight stream through a barred window up high. Grace 2 is lying motionless in the corner, bundled beneath a blanket.

I hope she's not dead.

"Grace," I whisper.

"E-Elliott?" she says meekly, raising her head. Her face is bruised.

"Are you okay?" I say, kneeling beside her. "I'm sorry they were rough with you, but I had to act the part."

"It's okay," she says. "I can take it. I knew it was you. Although I still can't believe it. What are you doing here?"

"I'll tell you later," I say. "Right now, we've got to get out of here."

"But you took my powers," she says. "I-I can't fly."

"That's temporary," I say. "Your powers will come back. But that's not going to help us now. We've got to get out of here. I have an idea. Hang on to your blanket."

I look over to the German Shepherd. "Dog-Gone, vanish."

He cocks another ear.

"Fine, I'll give you a bag of treats! Whatever!"

As soon as he disappears, I put my plan into action.

"Help!" I yell.

The door opens and the henchman burst in.

"My Lord?" says one.

"Are you okay?" says the other.

"I'm fine," I say. "But you're not." I concentrate hard and take away their super-strength. "Dog-Gone!"

Suddenly, both thugs are knocked to the ground. I grab Grace 2's hand and pull her out of the cell. As soon as Dog-Gone materializes next to us, I slam the door shut, locking the guards inside.

"Let's go," I say.

"But where?" Grace 2 asks.

"I know where your brother is," I say. "But we've got to get off this Earth. I need a ship."

Dog-Gone barks and nods his head.

"What's he saying?" Grace 2 asks.

"I think he wants us to follow him. Is that right?"

Dog-Gone 2 barks and then takes off.

Here we go again.

"We can't let anyone see you," I say to Grace 2. "Cover yourself in your blanket and follow that furball!"

We attract more strange looks, but I simply smile as Dog-Gone 2 leads us through a series of corridors, and out a side door.

Within minutes, we're in the woods, and Grace 2 and I collapse in a heap. We're out of breath, but we're safe, at least for the moment. Once Shadow Hawk 2 finds out what I've done, he'll be hot on my trail.

Dog-Gone 2 marches over to a thicket of tall bushes and barks again.

"What's he saying now?" Grace 2 asks.

The mutt paws at the thicket.

"I don't know," I say. "I think there's something behind there."

He barks again.

"Okay, okay," I say, walking over and sticking my gloved hands into the underbrush. As I push the thorny branches aside, I gasp out loud.

"What is it?" Grace 2 asks.

But, I don't have any words.

I wouldn't even know how to explain it.

It's my Freedom Ferry.

The one that vanished from my Earth.

Meta Profile

Name: Glory Girl 2
Role: Hero   Status: Active

VITALS:

Race: Human
Real Name: Grace Harkness
Height: 5'3"
Weight: 101 lbs
Eye Color: Blue
Hair Color: Brown

META POWERS:

Class: Flight
Power Level:
- **Considerable Flight**
- **Limited Super-Speed in combination with Earth's gravitational force.**

CHARACTERISTICS:

Combat	29
Durability	26
Leadership	40
Strategy	28
Willpower	57

NINE

I LOOK INTO A DARK MIRROR

We hop aboard the Freedom Ferry and blast off before Shadow Hawk 2 shows his beak.

I'm manning the controls, with Grace 2 and Dog-Gone 2 stuffed into the passenger seat. As we enter outer space, I relay everything I know about the Blur, which quite honestly isn't very much. But I'm guessing the appearance of my Freedom Ferry on Grace 2's world can only mean one thing—our two worlds are merging into one.

"So, why is this happening?" Grace 2 asks.

"Great question," I reply. "According to some intel I picked up back home, this whole thing started with the destruction of Order and Chaos on Arena World. Without those two bozos managing the rules of the multiverse, everything has gone whacko."

"Wonderful," Grace 2 says. "So, it's like survival of the fittest, galactic style."

"Seems that way," I say.

"Well, that stinks," she says. "By the way, are you ever planning on telling me where we're going?"

"Oh, sorry," I say. "I may be way off here, but based on the graffiti covering your brother's walls, I think he went to see the Watcher."

"The Watcher? Who's the Watcher?"

Another great question. I mean, who *is* the Watcher anyway? The last time I saw that weirdo was when the Zodiac took me to his planet to find out what happened to Aries. But the Watcher had no interest in answering that question. Instead, he tormented me about the location of the Orb of Oblivion—which he knew was inside my body!

But there's no need to get into that now. So, I give her the straight answer. "The Watcher is a cosmic entity who's fated to watch the events of the universe in exchange for immortality. He's also blind and several fries short of a Happy Meal."

"Wait," Grace 2 says. "The Watcher is blind? Isn't that like a total oxymoron."

"What did you call me?"

"Not you," she says. "An oxymoron is a figure of speech that's self-contradictory. Like a 'cruel kindness' or a 'living death.' I mean, how could anyone be called 'the

Watcher' and be blind?"

"Oh, I get it," I say. "Yeah, it's strange. He said he lost his sight because of something he did, we just never found out what. And something tells me I don't want to know."

"Okay," she says, "my creeper alert is now on high. Why would my brother want to see this Watcher dude anyway?"

"Well, *they* say—and please don't ask me who 'they' are—that the Watcher knows everything. So, I'm guessing your brother had questions and needed some answers."

Suddenly, the Freedom Flyer BEEPS and says, "You will arrive at Watcher World in 1000 meters."

"What kinds of questions?" she asks.

"How am I supposed to know? Maybe he wanted to know if Bigfoot is real, or why round pizza comes in a square box. You know," I say, looking up, "meaningful things… like… that…"

Something is wrong.

By now we should have visual confirmation of Watcher World. Yet, when I look out the window, there's nothing but black space and bright stars. I recheck the navigator.

"What's the matter?" Grace 2 asks.

"Um, I think we've lost a planet," I say. "And it's not a small planet."

"Could it be the Blur?" Grace asks.

I didn't think of that. I guess it could have been

wiped off the map by the Blur. But if that were the case, why would the navigator tell us we're almost there. According to TechnocRat, there's only one thing to do when your electronics go funky. So, I turn off the navigator and then turn it back on. When it reboots, I re-enter the coordinates.

"You will arrive at Watcher World in 700 meters," it says.

The navigator seems to be working fine. But when I look up I still don't see anything. Is this some sort of trick?

And then it hits me.

It's a test.

The last time I was here with the Zodiac, we had to pass through an imaginary asteroid belt. I guess after we cracked that illusion, he created a new one. This time he's pretending his planet is missing. Nice try.

"It's there," I say. "We just can't see it."

"Elliott," Grace 2 says nervously. "You sure about that?"

"Yep," I say, lowering the landing gear.

"400 meters," the navigator says.

"You're really, really sure?" Grace 2 says. "I mean, there's nothing down there. You can see that, right?"

"300 meters," the navigator says.

"Uh-huh," I say.

"200 meters."

"So, shouldn't you be pulling up now?" Grace asks.

"Uh-uh," I say.

Dog-Gone 2 howls.

"100 meters."

"Elliott!" Grace 2 screams.

"Brace yourself," I say, touching the Freedom Ferry down onto a patch of pure space. We THUMP hard and I step on the brakes. The Freedom Ferry bumps along before coming to a relatively smooth stop. "Told ya," I say, turning to my companions who are holding onto each other for dear life.

Suddenly, the area beneath us transforms from starry blackness into purplish, rocky terrain. Towering mountains appear all around, their peaks climbing high into the red sky and disappearing into thick, black clouds.

I'm back, and it's just as bleak as before.

Lightning flashes and Dog-Gone 2 whimpers.

"Well, this place looks like a party," Grace 2 says. "So, where are we supposed to go?"

Based on experience, we could easily spend days walking around lost. So, it's time for a shortcut. I punch a few commands into the navigator and within seconds it comes back with a direct hit.

"Stay seated," I warn, taking the Freedom Ferry airborne again. We break through the cloud cover and travel north for several miles. Then, I find what I'm looking for—a white structure sitting high atop a mountain.

The Watcher's sanctuary.

Nothing has changed from my last visit. There are still four marble columns supporting the marble roof, marble stairs leading up to the platform, and a giant, robed figure sitting in his oversized chair.

"That's him?" Grace 2 asks. "He's humongous!"

"Yeah, that's him," I say. "Look, I'm not sure how this is going to go down, so let me lead."

I set us down twenty yards away. As we exit, I start rehearsing what I'm going to say. I know we need to be super careful. I mean, anything can set this looney tune off. We need to be organized. We need to be commanding. We need to look like we mean business.

Then, I hear a trickling noise from behind me.

Turning around, I find Dog-Gone 2 with his hind leg in the air, soaking the Freedom Ferry's front tire.

"Seriously?"

"Give him a break," Grace 2 says. "It's been a long ride."

"Need anything else?" I ask. "Belly rub? Scratch under the chin? Flea removal?"

Dog-Gone 2 cocks an ear.

Freaking furball.

Time to lower my blood pressure. I take a deep breath, think calm thoughts, and then march up the staircase. When I reach the top, I'm face to face with a being I had hoped to never see again.

At first glance, the Watcher looks exactly like I remembered—tall, pale, and ugly. But then I realize something is off, I just can't figure out what.

"Watcher," I say, mustering all my confidence, "I've returned and we need your help. No games."

But the Watcher doesn't move a muscle. Instead, he just stares at me with his white eyes. It's like he's looking past me—through me.

I lower my voice and try again. "Watcher, I need your help."

But he doesn't respond. What's wrong with him? It's like he can't hear me, like he doesn't even know we're standing here.

Then, I realize what's different. The last time I was here he had this white, celestial glow around his body. And now, it's gone!

"Um, is everything okay?" Grace whispers.

"I'm not sure," I say, waving my arms. "Watcher? Are you okay? Can you hear me?"

"Oh, he can hear you," comes a kid's voice. "He's just not capable of answering you."

Looking up, I see a blond-haired, skinny kid sitting cross-legged on top of a boulder. He's wearing a red-and-blue costume with a 'no-symbol' across his chest.

I can't believe it! I've found him!

It's Elliott 2!

Dog-Gone 2 starts running in circles, his tail wagging with excitement.

"I see you, boy," Elliott 2 says, and then more coldly, "and you too, sister."

"What are you doing here, Elliott?" Grace 2 asks, unconsciously taking a step backward.

"I could ask the same of you," he says. "After all, few people know who the Watcher is, and fewer still know how to find him."

"I've been here before," I say. "Although the last time it was against my will. But you're here because you want to be. Why?"

"Why am I here?" Elliott 2 says with an unnerving smile. "Because I'm seeking knowledge. I want to know once and for all where *this* came from."

And then, he raises his right hand, and what's resting in his palm sends a chill down my spine.

It's the Orb of Oblivion!

I was right! There is a second one!

"What's that?" Grace 2 asks.

"Precisely, dear sister," he says. "The object has a name, but not an identity. At least, not one I can get it to tell me. And oh, have I tried. Isn't that right, Orb?"

The Orb gives off a weak glow.

My stomach sinks as I watch him shift the Orb from hand to hand. All of my fantasies about Elliott 2 being a victim of the Orb go completely out the window. The Orb hasn't exerted its will over him, he's exerted his will over the Orb! He's in absolute and total control. And that means all of his actions were done of his own free will.

He's pure evil.

"At first, the only thing I could squeeze out of the

all-mighty Orb of Oblivion was an image of this guy," he says, nodding to the Watcher. "So, let's just say I had to dig a little harder. Finally, the Orb gave up the Watcher's name and location. It took me a few months to plot out how to get here—and the journey took far longer than I imagined—but we arrived just in time because my Freedom Ferry is out of fuel. And then, after all of that travel, we get here and the bald guy won't answer any of my questions. So, I put him on a time out."

"A time out?" I blurt. "You put a cosmic entity on a time out?"

"Yep," he says. "I don't like to be bored, and you'd be surprised at how easily you get bored when you can do anything."

Suddenly, he leaps down from the boulder and lands between the Watcher and me. For a moment, I'm taken aback. His face, his body, his posture—everything looks like me! Except, of course, for his hair color. It's like I'm staring into a mirror. But unfortunately, I'm not.

He looks me up and down. "You're quite boring, aren't you?"

"Excuse me?" I say.

"You live a pathetic life, don't you?" he continues. "On the outside, you pretend to be a great hero. But on the inside, you're shaking like a leaf. You're a coward. A poser. Am I right?"

"No!"

"Are you sure?" he continues, holding the Orb in

front of his face. "Because I know I'm right. I can feel it."

I gaze deeply into the white, pulsating Orb. I'm mesmerized by it—lost in it, when…

"Save me," comes a tiny cry inside my head.

The voice is feeble, yet familiar. Who?

"Save me. Save us all."

It's the Orb! It's talking to me!

But how? I thought Elliott 2 mastered it?

"So," Elliott 2 says, snapping me back to reality, "What's a brave hero like you doing in a dead-end place like this?"

"I was looking for something," I say. "But now I've found it."

At first, he looks confused, but then he glances down at the Orb and the smirk disappears from his face. "This? You were looking for this? Really? I can't imagine what for, but if you think I'm just going to give it to you, you're more delusional than I thought."

This is it. If I don't get the Orb of Oblivion away from him now, I've got zero chance of stopping Ravager from eating my world.

I look him dead in the eyes.

"Oh, I never expected you to give it to me," I say coolly. "That's why I'm going to take it from you."

Meta Profile

Name: Epic Zero 2
Role: Villain   Status: Active

VITALS:

Race: Human
Real Name: Elliott Harkness
Height: 4'8"
Weight: 89 lbs
Eye Color: Brown
Hair Color: Blond

META POWERS:

Class: Meta Manipulation
Powers Level:

- Extreme Power Negation and Manipulation
- Vulnerable to non-Meta attack

CHARACTERISTICS:

Combat	25	
Durability	12	
Leadership	55	
Strategy	65	
Willpower	77	

TEN

I FIGHT MY OWN SHADOW

Somehow, I always knew it would come down to this.

I mean, how else was I going to walk away with the Orb of Oblivion? I guess deep down I kind of wished a second Orb didn't exist. That way, I'd never have to face what I'm about to face now.

Which is probably the end of my life.

So, let's get realistic and break down my chances for success. One, we're both scrawny kids, so we're even there. Two, we both have Meta Manipulation powers— even again. Three, he's got the Orb of Oblivion, the most powerful weapon in the universe, while I've got a serious case of anxiety.

Major advantage to him.

Looks like I'm doomed.

I mean, how can I possibly win? He just put the Watcher down for the count—a freaking cosmic being! I'm no oddsmaker, but I'd say I've got a better chance of finding a unicorn than beating him.

Well, at least Grace 2 is here to help.

Suddenly, Elliott 2 extends his right hand and commands, "Sleep!"

Grace 2 crumples to the ground like a rag doll.

Okay, now I've got a better chance of finding a whole herd of unicorns.

Dog-Gone 2 bares his teeth and growls at me.

"Down, boy, he's mine," Elliott 2 says, the Orb pulsating in his hands. "You know, I always suspected there was some goody-two-shoes version of me out there who never realized his own power. And now here you are."

"Lucky me," I say. Great, now I'm being insulted by my own double. Honestly, I'm having a hard time matching what I'm hearing with what I'm seeing. I mean, he looks exactly like me, yet our personalities are like night and day. My only chance is to distract him until I can figure out what to do.

"So, Dr. Sunshine," I say sarcastically. "What made you so happy-go-lucky? I know a bit about the Orb of Oblivion and how it feeds on your innermost desires, but even a boring, goody-two-shoes like me managed to resist it."

"You want a medal or something?" he says with a

laugh. "I can tell we aren't so different. Before I discovered the Orb, my life pretty much stunk like yours. No one paid any attention to me. I was considered a nuisance—a pest. But when opportunity knocked, I didn't close the door. I opened it—embraced it. And look at me now."

Yeah, I'm looking at him, and he's rotten to the core. My eyes dart around for something—anything—to help me. But all I see are purple rocks, orange plants—and the Freedom Ferry! If I can get to the ship, then maybe I can blast out of here. But then again, I can't just leave Grace 2 here. Plus, I really need that orb.

I'm stuck!

"I'd feel terrible if you came all this way and left empty-handed," he says, flashing a menacing smile. "Since you want the power of the Orb so badly, let me give it to you."

Oh, n—

Suddenly, there's a sharp, stabbing pain in my head.

He's entered my mind!

My brain feels like it's being stepped on! Squashed!

I drop to my knees.

He's trying to overpower me! If he breaks through he'll control my mind, then there's no telling what he'll do. I can't let him in. I muster every ounce of negation power and push back.

"Maybe you resisted the Orb on your world," he says, through gritted teeth, "but you won't be able to resist me."

The pressure is overwhelming. It feels like my head is going to explode! I've got to get him out. I push back harder.

"You're strong," he says, with a hint of surprise. "Stronger than anyone I've taken over before. But don't worry, I'll break you down soon enough."

Suddenly, I'm flat on the ground. With all of my energy focused on defending myself, I have no control over the rest of my body. I'm holding him at bay, but for how long? He's way too strong!

"Use me," comes a feeble voice inside my head.

What? Who's that?

"Use me," it repeats, a little louder.

The Orb? But how's it talking to me? Can't Elliott 2 hear it?

"No," it says. *"I barely managed to shield my innermost conscious from him. But if you want to live, you must use me now."*

"H-How?"

"All you need to do is stop pushing back," it says. *"Just open your mind, let me inside, and I'll do the rest."*

"Let you inside? Are you bonkers? As soon as I do that he'll take over and I'll be eating baby food for the rest of my life!"

"If you don't use me," it says. *"You're as good as dead."*

"You're weakening," Elliott 2 says. "I'm almost through."

And he's right! My head feels like it's being drilled in half by a jackhammer.

"Use me!" the Orb pleads again.

I'm getting loopy. Dizzy. Images of Mom, Dad, and Grace flash before my eyes. If I can't find a way to defeat him, they're as good as dead.

The pain is so intense!

I-I've got no other choice!

I close my eyes… and then I let go.

Instantly, the pressure releases.

An intense wave of energy rushes through my body. I open my eyes, and it's like every fiber of my being is on hyper-alert. I can see the tiny pores in Elliott 2's skin. I can hear Dog-Gone 2's neck hair blowing in the breeze. I can feel thousands of invisible molecules bouncing off my skin.

I've never felt so alive. So… powerful. It's like I've gone from Zero to… to… Meta 4?

"Hey!" Elliott 2 cries, looking at the orb in his hand. "What happened? It's not working?"

Despite the energy coursing through my veins, it feels like I'm moving in slow motion. Like I'm stuck in molasses. Like I'm having an out-of-body experience.

Elliott 2's brown eyes widen as he realizes the Orb of Oblivion has left the round object in his hands—and entered my body.

"Now," the Orb says. *"Strike now."*

While I'd love nothing more than to go off on some epic monologue about good triumphing over evil, my body is being compelled to do something else. My eyes shut and one overriding thought fills my mind.

NO. MORE.

Then, my eyes pop open and a wave of strange, orange energy comes pouring out, washing over Elliott 2.

Huh? Where'd that come from?

But before I can figure that out, the energy dissipates, and Elliott 2 is on his hands and knees, mumbling, "N-no. My... powers."

And then I realize what happened.

The Orb negated his powers.

Permanently.

He's a Zero.

"Y-You did this to me," he says, rising to his feet. He throws the useless orb to the ground. "You took the Orb of Oblivion's power from me. Give it back. Give it back to me, or I'll kill you."

"Now," the Orb says. *"Finish him."*

"What? No!"

"Do not block me," the Orb urges. *"Open up to me."*

I watch as Elliott 2 picks up a sharp rock. "The Orb is mine. Not yours. Mine!"

Dog-Gone 2 joins his side and barks threateningly.

My arm extends magically and I hear my self saying, "STAY!"

Dog-Gone 2 freezes like a statue.

Elliott 2 springs towards me, the rock held menacingly over his head, when suddenly, a streaking blue fist connects squarely with his jaw.

Elliott 2 flies backward into a rock, and then face plants to the ground.

"Enough, little brother," Grace 2 says, rubbing her knuckles. "We've all had enough."

Dog-Gone 2 whimpers and I release him from my hold. He scampers to his master's side and starts licking his face, but Elliott 2 doesn't move. He's out cold.

"You should have finished him," the Orb says. *"You still can, while he's defenseless. You need to open everything to me."*

"Quiet," I command, trying to shut the Orb down, but I can tell things are going to be different this time around. This Orb is much stronger than the one I had before.

I pick the sphere up off the ground. The Orb of Oblivion is mine again. Heaven help us all.

"You okay?" Grace 2 asks.

"I'm... not sure," I say. "You know, we never found out why he came here in the first place. But I've got this funny feeling we're running out of—"

"—time?" rumbles a deep voice behind me.

I spin around to find the Watcher fully conscious in his chair. Man, I can't catch a break around here.

"Time, Elliott Harkness, is your greatest enemy."

Great. Just what I need right now.

"I've got no clue what you're saying, but I know we've got no time to figure out your crazy riddles. So, be a pal and just tell me what you know."

"What I know," the Watcher says, tilting his head

towards the stars, "is that everything is about to end. And it is all my fault."

"Your fault?" I say. "What are you talking about?"

"In exchange for immortality, I have sat here for countless millennia witnessing the events of the multiverse. Over that expanse of time, I have watched billions of creatures become parents, and in turn, their children became parents, and so on. I sat, and I watched, and I wondered. What was the purpose of my bargain? What would I have to show for it? Who would I ever share it with?"

"Um, okay," I say. Where is this going?

"By nature, I was not born a cosmic being, but I was granted a measure of cosmic power. And though it was forbidden for me to exercise this power, century by century, decade by decade, my will became weaker and weaker. And then, one day... it broke, and I violated my solemn oath to be an impartial observer."

I glance at Grace 2 who's eyes are bugged out of her head. Whatever's coming next is gonna be a doozy.

"So," the Watcher continues, "I created a child."

"You what?" I blurt out.

"At first, I was able to mask its existence. But as it grew larger, so did its appetite. I tried to satiate it, but it soon became impossible. In time, it wandered away, looking to alleviate its hunger pains."

Hunger pains?

Wait a minute? No way...

"Y-You mean your child is… is…," I stutter.

"Ravager," the Watcher says. "My child is Ravager."

I feel my jaw hit my toes. I immediately think of all those innocent people, all of those helpless creatures—billions of them—destroyed by Ravager, simply because he was hungry.

"After a while," the Watcher continues, "it grew too large for even my powers to conceal. It was destructive, and soon its presence became known to the cosmic regulators, Order and Chaos. They reprimanded me, and as a consequence of interfering in the affairs of the multiverse, they took away my sight, but not my immortality. Thus, I have been punished to sit here in darkness until the end of eternity."

"You should be punished!" I yell. "You're responsible for all of this death and destruction! All because you wanted a stupid kid?"

"Yes," the Watcher says, lowering his head. "As its father, I swore I would protect it at all costs. I begged Order and Chaos to spare it, to use it in any manner they pleased, but to let it live. And use it they did—in their twisted games. That is, until they were destroyed on Arena World and Ravager was set free once again."

"Yeah," I say. "Free to eat more worlds like mine."

"This is my greatest regret," the Watcher says. "I became a father to realize the joys of parenthood, but instead I have unleashed an evil so dark it robs the multiverse of the same light. Ravager may be my child, but I know it must be destroyed."

"And how are you going to do that?" I ask.

"I may be the one who created it," the Watcher says, "but I am not destined to destroy it."

Great. Well if it's not him then who…

Oh, no.

"Elliott Harkness, once again you are the Orb Master. You possess the final Orb of Oblivion, the most powerful weapon in the multiverse."

"Annnnd, what exactly am I supposed to do with it?" I ask, dreading the answer.

"Is it not obvious?" the Watcher says, peering through me with his dead, white pupils. "You must take the Orb of Oblivion to Ravager's brain and blow it up."

Meta Profile

Name: Watcher
Role: Cosmic Entity   Status: Active

VITALS:

Race: Inapplicable
Real Name: Watcher
Height: 10'0"
Weight: Unknown
Eye Color: White
Hair Color: Bald

META POWERS:

Class: Inapplicable
Power Level: Incalculable

- Observes all events in the universe
- Cannot interfere in any way, or will suffer dire consequences

CHARACTERISTICS:

Combat	Inapplicable
Durability	Inapplicable
Leadership	Inapplicable
Strategy	Inapplicable
Willpower	Inapplicable

ELEVEN

I ENTER BIZARRO WORLD

"**E**lliott? Are you okay?"

I hear my name, and I know I should respond, but I can't. I'm completely numb.

Everything spins as Grace 2 guides the Freedom Ferry into a barrel roll. I feel weightless for a moment, the seat belt digging into my chest, but then we're right-side-up and gravity takes hold again. Grace 2 is pushing the Freedom Ferry to the max, and rightly so because after the Watcher's shocking revelation we're running out of time—time to stop Ravager.

We didn't have a holding cell for Elliott 2, so we left him on Watcher World for now. And quite frankly, I couldn't think of a more fitting punishment than being trapped listening to the Watcher blow hot air. At least

Dog-Gone 2 stayed behind to keep them company.

What I can't understand is why all this bad stuff keeps happening to me? It's like there's some giant "kick me" sign on my back. Look, I knew I needed the Orb to stop Ravager—that's why I came here in the first place— but I always pictured using it from a distance, not up close and personal. I mean, even if I somehow manage to blow up Ravager's brain, won't I blow up with it?

It's like a suicide mission.

Fabulous.

"There is another way," the Orb says.

Speaking of fabulous…

"Quiet," I say. *"I'm not taking advice from you."*

"You would listen to that blind fool over me?" it says. *"His path leads to your demise. My path leads to your ascension. Your crowning as king of the multiverse!"*

"No dice," I say. *"And shut your trap."*

I try silencing it. Pushing it down. But it's not moving.

"You can't control me," it says. *"I'm not like the other one. Just wait, you'll see."*

Great. Can't wait.

The Orb. The Blur. Ravager. It's way too much. And, of course, it's all up to me.

And that's what worries me the most.

I take a deep breath and exhale.

I think back to Elliott 2's words. I can put on a brave face and pretend to be a great hero. But I know the truth.

I'm not superhero enough for this.

I mean, if I couldn't even jump into a sewer to face Alligazer, how am I ever going to do this? Poor Makeshift paid the ultimate price for my mistake. Now I'm supposed to take on a nebulous, globe-eating monstrosity with billions of lives at stake? Who's kidding who?

I just want to crawl into a hole and hide. Maybe Captain Justice 2 had it right. Maybe some people aren't cut out to be heroes.

"Prepare to submerge," Grace 2 says.

"What?" I say. I was so lost in thought I didn't notice we'd already made it back into Earth 2's atmosphere. Looking down, I realize we're making a beeline for a large body of water. "Um, what's that?"

"The Atlantic Ocean," she says.

"And why are we aimed at it?"

"To get reinforcements," she says. Then, she flicks a few switches and the Freedom Ferry converts to amphibious mode. "Hang on."

I brace myself as we jackknife through the water, and thousands of tiny bubbles blanket the windshield. I wait for her to level off, but she's not straightening up. I check the navigator and realize we're 2,000 feet deep and still diving! I'm not sure the ship can hold up under this kind of pressure. "We're too deep!"

"Relax," Grace 2 says calmly. "We do this all the time."

All the time? I've got no idea what she's talking

about, when suddenly, the bubbles clear, and I'm staring at something humungous sitting on the ocean floor.

It's an underwater fortress!

It's big, and gray, and divided into three sections connected by airlocks. It looks thick—like it's forged from alloyed steel. On top are several rotating radar dishes and the largest antenna I've ever seen. Rows of portholes line each compartment, indicating there are multiple levels inside. The entire structure stands proudly on four giant, metal legs burrowed deep into the ground.

"What's that?" I ask.

"The Hydrostation," Grace 2 says. "Hydro means water, but phonetically it's Hide-ro, as in hidden. Get it? Not a bad name for the secret headquarters of the Freedom Force."

That's the secret headquarters of the Freedom Force 2? Now I realize why no one has heard of the Waystation around here. Because there is no Waystation. It's a Hydrostation!

We cruise around the building's perimeter, stopping in front of a giant hatch door that slides welcomingly open. Grace 2 maneuvers us inside and the door shuts behind us. Large, rotating wheels lock us in tight.

We're inside, but still hovering in seawater, making me wonder how we're actually going to get out of the ship. But that's quickly answered when large pumps in the hangar floor kick on, expelling the water and gently lowering us to the floor. Then, giant fans hanging from the ceiling take care of any remaining moisture.

The hangar is bone dry. Pretty impressive.

"Are you ready to meet the rest of the team?" she asks, popping open the Freedom Ferry door.

"As ready as I'll ever be," I say.

Grace 2 exits first and is greeted by a motley crew of costumed heroes. Ms. Understood 2 leads the pack, running up and giving Grace 2 a big hug. "Grace, what happened? We thought you were captured. We were about to come rescue you."

"I was," Grace 2 says. "But Elliott rescued me first."

"Elliott?" Ms. Understood 2 says.

Before my foot hits the ground she wraps me up in a big hug. "I never thought I'd see you again," she says. "But I'm so glad you're here. Thank you for saving her. I guess we owe you twice now."

"My pleasure," I say. It's still weird seeing a version of my mom with blond hair instead of brown, but that's why I think of her as Mom 2. Then, I notice a small gray rat sitting on her shoulder that could only be this world's version of TechnocRat.

"That seals it," he says, staring at the Freedom Ferry with his beady little eyes and pulling on a long whisker. "My theory is confirmed."

I've got no clue what he's talking about. But what interests me more is the skinny, spikey-haired man standing behind them. He's wearing a green costume with gold electric volts that meet in the center of his chest.

Taser? He's a good guy?

Then, to his right, comes a small, thick-set man with an orange costume and a mohawk. Could it be? Without thinking, I run over and throw my arms around him.

"Makeshift! I'm so happy to see you alive!"

He looks down at me funny and says, "Um, do I know you?"

Suddenly, I realize this isn't the Makeshift from my world. It's Makeshift 2! I back up, my cheeks flush with embarrassment. "Sorry, I thought you were someone else. It's a long story."

"I bet," he says.

I take in the ragtag group of heroes standing before me. This is all that's left of the Freedom Force 2? If so, I don't know how we're going to defeat Ravager. We need more help. Major help.

"Mind if I lend a hand?" comes a deep voice.

I turn to find a dark-haired man in a red, white, and blue uniform stepping out of the airlock—the scales of justice insignia stretched across his chest. It's Captain Justice 2! His beard is trimmed and his hair is cut short.

"Dad?" Grace 2 says. "What are you doing here?"

Dad 2 puts his hand on my shoulder. "Someone reminded me of what it means to be a hero. It doesn't matter what powers you have, or how good you are at using them, being a hero is about never giving up, no matter the odds."

"So, you're back?" Grace 2 asks.

He looks at Mom 2 and smiles. "Yes, I've rejoined the Freedom Force."

Grace 2 gives him a big hug. "That's the best news ever."

"So, where exactly have you guys been?" Mom 2 asks.

Grace 2 and I look at each other.

"Speaking of long stories," she says. "How about we give you the quick version over some jelly doughnuts? I'm starving!"

***

After recapping our crazy adventures in the Galley, we take a much-needed bathroom break and then reconvene in the Mission Room. As I enter, I marvel at how eerily identical the Hydrostation is to the Waystation. Some of the rooms are on different levels, but both headquarters have a Combat Room, a Monitor Room, a Lounge, a Galley, a Vault, a Lab, and, of course, living quarters.

The Freedom Force 2 take their seats around the large, circular conference table. There are twelve seats in all, so I hop into one of the empty ones.

"So, Elliott," Mom 2 starts, "from what I understand, the entire multiverse is collapsing into one, there's a giant mist coming to swallow your Earth, you're carrying the most powerful weapon in the universe, and my son and his dog are stranded on a distant planet being watched by a cosmic, blind babysitter. Did I miss anything?"

"Nope, that pretty much sums it up," I say.

"So, what's our next move?" Dad 2 asks.

"I need to get back home," I say. "As quickly as possible."

"And how are you going to do that?" he asks.

"Well, my friend Wind Walker got me here, and he told me to call him when I want to go back. So, I guess I should give him a shout. I suggest you cover your ears."

The heroes look at one another and then comply. I stand up, inhale deeply, and yell, "WIND WALKER!"

But there's nothing.

From the stares I'm getting, I've clearly identified myself as a crazy person. "Sorry," I say. "That's how I got him last time."

Before Wind Walker took off, he told me he was trying to figure out the Blur. He said that hopefully he could come back for me. So, if he's not here, something must have gone terribly wrong. And now there's no way for me to get back home.

My legs feel wobbly and I slump back into my chair. I can't believe I got this far, and now I'm stuck. My family, my friends, they're all doomed.

"I… I failed my mission," I say.

"Perhaps," TechnocRat 2 says, scampering to the center of the table, "but perhaps not. Follow me." Then, he leaps onto the floor and runs into the hallway.

We follow him through the Hydrostation until he bolts into a familiar-looking sunken chamber—his laboratory.

Apparently, this TechnocRat isn't any neater than mine. He's got all the beakers, vials, Bunsen burners, microscopes, and other assorted equipment my rat does, but there's one noticeable difference. Smack-dab in the center of the room is a giant sphere.

"What's with the hamster ball?" Taser 2 asks.

"Very funny," TechnocRat 2 says, climbing up a mini-ramp and parking himself in front of a computer. "I call it the Jump Ship."

"Also known as big trouble," Grace 2 whispers.

"You see," TechnocRat 2 continues, punching computer keys with his paws, "I've been picking up some odd readings in our atmosphere." Then, he points at me with his tail. "The fact that he's standing here is astonishing in its own right—although I presume this Wind Walker character transported him here through a wormhole. But what's more astonishing is the vehicle they arrived in. That Freedom Ferry is from his universe, and it entered our universe on its own."

"So?" Taser 2 says. "Get to the point, cheese head."

"So, according to my analytical models, at this very moment, his universe and our universe are literally sitting on top of one another."

"What?" Makeshift 2 says.

It's the Blur. It's happening to us. Like, right now!

"Our two universes are in a state of pre-merger," TechnocRat 2 says. "At any time, the molecules could shift and one of our universes will be completely and totally wiped out."

"Well, that's comforting," Taser 2 says.

"If I could have everyone step inside the Jump Ship. Except you, Captain, you'll need to wait here."

We scramble up the ramp and inside the strange sphere. It's not as roomy as it looks from the outside, but at least it's translucent, so it feels larger than it is.

"Okay, TechnocRat," Dad 2 says. "What's going on here?"

"The Jump Ship is constructed entirely from unstable molecules that don't conform to the traditional rules of our universe. So, if my calculations are correct, when propelled with the right amount of force we may be able to exit our universe and enter Elliott's universe. All we need is for our resident strongman to pick us up, and pitch the fastest fastball ever recorded."

"And if your calculations are wrong?" Mom 2 asks.

"Captain Justice will have a lot of cleaning up to do."

"Lovely," I say.

"Is there any way I can join you after?" Dad 2 asks.

"I'm afraid not, Captain," TechnocRat 2 says. "This may be the last time we see each other."

"Dad, no!" Grace 2 cries.

"Sorry, darling," Dad 2 says, lifting the enormous

sphere with one hand. "But as I've come to realize, being a hero is about sacrifice, no matter how painful the consequences may be."

And then, with tremendous strength, he stretches back and hurls us towards the far wall.

Meta Profile
The Freedom Force 2

Taser 2

Class: Energy Manipulator
Meta: ▮

Glory Girl 2

Class: Flight
Meta: ▮▮

Captain Justice 2

Class: Super-Strength
Meta: ▮▮▮

Ms. Understood 2

Class: Psychic
Meta: ▮▮▮

TechnocRat 2

Class: Super-Intellect
Meta: ▮▮▮▮

Makeshift 2

Class: Energy Manipulator
Meta: ▮

TWELVE

I ATTEND A FAMILY REUNION GONE WRONG

Ripping through the fabric of the universe is deafening stuff.

It sort of sounds like splitting your pants—not that it's ever happened to me—but magnified a million times. Inside the Jump Ship, we're smashing into each other like kernels in a popcorn machine, and I'm pretty sure at one point a rat tail went up my nose!

This whole experiment is a crazy gamble. Our only hope is that TechnocRat 2's unstable molecules do their job. In hindsight, I probably should have asked a few more questions before putting my life at risk. Like, what's the probability this will actually work? But it's too late now.

Looking through the exterior of the Jump Ship is like looking through frosted glass. I can tell it's dark outside—like we're spinning through nothingness—but that's about it. Who knows, maybe we're already dead? Boy, wouldn't that solve all my problems, at least in the short run?

I think I'm gonna be sick.

"Are you enjoying yourself?"

"Not now," I answer in my mind. *"Please."*

"You can still rule," the Orb says. *"Just say the word."*

"Here are two words," I say, *"shut it."*

"Suit yourself," it says. *"Hope you don't barf."*

CRACK! comes a sharp, bone-rattling noise, and suddenly, we're bathed in light.

"Yes!" TechnocRat 2 cries. "We're through!"

The Jump Ship skips along with reckless abandon. Every time we bump the ground it feels like a sucker punch to the gut. Arms and legs are flailing about everywhere. Finally, we break into a smooth roll, cruising along for what seems like miles before SMACKING into something solid that stops our momentum cold.

I'm lying face down, my nose pressed into the bottom of the sphere. Propping myself on my elbows, I take in the scene around me. The Jump Ship looks like a hospital ward: Grace 2 has a bloody nose, Taser 2 is nursing his left arm, Mom 2 has a bruised eye, and Makeshift 2 is hugging TechnocRat 2 like he's a teddy bear.

"Is everyone okay?" TechnocRat 2 squeaks out.

He's answered with moans and groans.

My neck is so sore it feels like I've got whiplash, but I don't have time for pain. Right now, I just need to know if we made it back to my universe. There's only one way to find out. I look around hopelessly for the door before I realize it's spun to the top of the Jump Ship.

"We need to make a plan," I hear TechnocRat 2 say.

A plan. Right, sounds good. I get up on my feet, and step on Makeshift 2's back. "Hey!" he shouts, but I ignore him, and reach up for the latch.

"Elliott, wait!" I hear Mom 2 say.

The latch is outside my reach. I just need to stretch a little further... a little more...

Got it!

I pull down, and the door opens inwards. With considerable effort I swing up, grabbing the side of the opening, and haul myself up. When I'm halfway out of the Jump Ship, I balance myself and take a look around.

Hey, I know those buildings!

That's Main Street! There's the ice cream shop! The police station! I'm back in Keystone City!

My Keystone City!

We did it! We really did—

"Duck!" cries the Orb.

Without thinking, I drop into the Jump Ship, just as something large WHOOSHES overhead!

Luckily, the heroes catch me before I break my legs.

"Elliott?" Grace 2 says. "You look as white as a ghost? What was it?"

I'm not really sure.

I need to get back up there.

"Elliott?" she says.

"Lift me up," I say.

This time, Makeshift 2 kneels and I climb up onto his shoulders. He pushes me up and I wiggle my way out of the Jump Ship. I look into the sky.

It's filled with objects.

Floating objects.

They're not clouds. Or airplanes. Or birds.

They're warships.

Skelton warships.

Hundreds of them.

"Get out here now!" I order. "We're under attack!"

Grace 2 flies up and pulls me out of the Jump Ship. The other heroes scramble out and join us on the ground.

"Holy guacamole!" TechnocRat 2 says.

"Is that what I think it is?" Grace 2 says.

"There's too many of them!" Taser 2 says.

"We don't have much time," Mom 2 says. "We need to get every civilian to safety. Quick, let's assign roles."

The heroes converge, but I can't concentrate on anything they're saying. My mind is completely somewhere else. I mean, what are all these Skelton warships doing here? The last time I saw the Skelton Emperor, Arena World was breaking into a billion pieces and I thought we had an understanding. I wanted nothing to do with him, and since I didn't have the Orb of Oblivion, he had no use for me.

He wouldn't know I had another Orb, would he? It's not possible. So, what's his fleet doing here?

"Elliott?" comes a female voice in my brain. *"Is that you?"*

Spinning around, I find a colorful group of heroes heading our way. It's the Freedom Force!

My Freedom Force!

They stop a few feet short of us and stare at the strange crew around me.

"Epic Zero," Dad says, his fists clenched, "are you in danger?"

"No, sir," I say. "These are my friends. They're the Freedom Force, but from a different universe."

"Say what?" Grace says. "What are you talking about?"

"Look," I say, "I know this is gonna sound weird, but our two universes are like, right on top of each other. In fact, they're merging together and only one of them is going to survive because of a cosmic crisis called the Blur. But trust me, that's not even our biggest problem right now. See, there's this galactic monster on its way to eat our planet. And now, for some reason, we're about to be invaded by Skelton. Are you guys following me?"

"You mean, like, to the insane asylum?" Grace asks.

"Absolutely fascinating," TechnocRat says, rocketing

over us in his jetpack to get a closer look at the Jump Ship. He turns to his gray double. "Unstable molecules?"

"Yes," TechnocRat 2 says excitedly. "I've been working with them for over a decade, but only in a laboratory setting. You wouldn't believe how difficult it is to get unidentified—"

"—atomic nuclei to cooperate?" TechnocRat finishes.

"Great," Grace says. "Now we've got techno-babble in stereo. Anyway, are these weirdos you're with for real? And who in their right mind thought I'd look good as a brunette?"

"Hey!" Grace 2 says. "You're right, Elliott, she is rude!"

"Rude?" Grace says. "I'll show you rude!"

"Isn't that Taser?" Blue Bolt asks. "Isn't he a villain?"

"If you're looking for villains," Taser 2 says, pointing to Shadow Hawk, "Just look at him."

"You got a problem?" Shadow Hawk says menacingly.

"Yeah," Makeshift 2 says, stepping forward. "How'd you like a one-way ticket to Exile?"

"Makeshift?" Dad says. "You're alive!"

"Yeah," Makeshift 2 says, powering up. "Which is more than I can say for you."

"Whoa! Whoa! Time out!" I say, stepping in between the teams. This isn't exactly the reunion I was hoping for.

They're at each other's throats! "Look, we're all heroes here."

"Ell—I mean, Epic Zero," Mom says firmly, "I'm sure your new friends are lovely people, but can you please tell me exactly where you've been? Clearly, disappearing for days on end without communication isn't an issue for you, but for those of us responsible for your well-being it's been a little nerve-wracking."

Oh, boy. I know that tone. "Didn't you see my note?" I ask.

"What note?" she asks, her arms crossed and foot tapping.

"The note I left for you in... TechnocRat's incredibly messy laboratory. Right, sorry."

"We'll finish this discussion later," Dad says. "Now, about these friends of yours..."

Okay, I'm in big trouble, but we're all toast if I can't stop them from being so distracted by each other that we fail to focus on what matters most.

Distracted? Hang on. That's it!

O. M. G.

I know what the Skelton are doing here!

"You finally figured it out, huh, genius?" says the Orb.

"Don't start," I respond.

"We can take them," it says. *"You have all the power you need. It's standing all around you."*

"What? What does that mean?"

Suddenly, there's an intense blast of light,

temporarily blinding us. Shielding my eyes, I look up.

Hovering above us is the Herald!

"Good day, heroes," he says.

"Um, is that the galactic monster you were telling us about?" Grace asks.

"No," I say.

"Then, who is he?"

"I vote for bad news," Taser 2 says.

"I am called the Herald," he says. "So, we meet again, little hero."

Of course, more insults.

"Wait," Grace says. "You know this guy?"

"Yep," I say.

"Is he a good guy?" she asks.

"Nope," I say.

"Fabulous," she says.

"I told you I would return," the Herald says.

"And I see you brought friends," I say.

"Ah, yes," he says, looking around. "When I required assistance to destroy Earth it did not take the Skelton long to sign up. In fact, they were quite motivated. I knew they would be."

"Why are they here?" I ask. "You didn't need them when you helped Ravager destroy Protaraan."

"Protaraan did not have heroes," he says. "I have found that heroes tend to interfere where they do not belong."

"I thought so," I say. "So, the Skelton are here to

distract us while you do your dirty work, huh? I guess you're scared we'll stop you."

"Oh, you will not stop me," the Herald says. "I just prefer not to be slowed down."

I look him dead in the eyes. "We'll do a lot more than slow you down."

"You amuse me, little hero," he says. "But you cannot slow, what you cannot catch."

Then, he takes off in a flash, leaving a fiery trail behind him.

"I'll get him!" both Grace's say simultaneously.

But before they can move, there's a THUNDERING noise from above.

The Skelton warships are heading right for us!

It's begun.

Meta Profile

Name: Orb of Oblivion 2
Role: Cosmic Entity   Status: Active

VITALS:

Race: Inapplicable
Real Name: Inapplicable
Height: 4.0 inches
Weight: 7.0 oz
Eye Color: Inapplicable
Hair Color: Inapplicable

META POWERS:

Class: Inapplicable
Power Level: Inapplicable

- A parasite that seeks out unfulfilled desires and feeds off of them
- Limitless power—can do whatever its host imagines

CHARACTERISTICS:

Combat   Inapplicable
Durability   Inapplicable
Leadership   Inapplicable
Strategy   Inapplicable
Willpower   Inapplicable

THIRTEEN

I TRY TO CATCH FIRE

"Freedom Force—it's Fight Time!"

I watch Dad rally the troops as hundreds of Skelton warships race towards us. I wish I could stay and help, but I've got to stop the Herald. The only problem is how?

He's fast and already has a big head start. There's no Freedom Ferry to jump into, and I certainly can't fly.

"Are you sure about that?" the Orb says.

"I think I'd know if I could fly?" I answer.

"That's the old you talking," it says. *"Not the new you."*

"What are you babbling about?"

But there's no time to figure that out because the Skelton are on top of us. Master Mime encases us in a bubble of purple energy, blocking the barrage of laser fire, but his shield is taking a pounding. I can see Master Mime struggling to keep it intact. I'm not sure how long he'll hold up. In fact, I'm not sure how we're going to survive this!

"We need to draw them away from the city!" Mom says. "Captain Justice, Master Mime, Blue Bolt, you provide cover. Everyone else follow me."

Suddenly, the two Graces grab my arms and lift me into the air. "Let's go, Bro," my sister says.

"Wait!" I yell, "Put me down!" But they're not listening. They're carrying me away—in the opposite direction of the Herald!

"Stop squirming and relax," Grace 2 says. "We've got to get you safe, then we'll deal with that fireball."

But they don't understand. The Skelton aren't the real danger here—it's the Herald!

I watch as Dad, Master Mime, and Blue Bolt stand their ground against the advancing armada. Dad is grabbing anything he can get his hands on—abandoned cars, street poles, trash cans—and launching them into the heart of the Skelton formation. Blue Bolt is running in circles, kicking up tornadoes that catch Skelton warships and spin them back into space. Master Mime created a giant purple tennis racket and is backhanding warships left and right.

But there's just too many of them.

Dozens are slipping through the cracks.

They'll be on us soon.

"Now!" the Orb says.

"Now what?"

"Open your mind," it says. *"Use me."*

"No!"

"Last time you gave in to me," it says. *"But then you pulled back. Let me in. Let me in completely. It's the only way."*

Despite my objections, I feel myself being drawn to its power—it's like an itch I need to scratch deep inside my brain. I feel it pulling me. Luring me in.

I try to resist, but it's so hard. Then, I realize the Orb has simply been biding its time, patiently waiting for the moment where I need it so desperately that I have no choice but to let it completely occupy every nook and cranny of my mind.

I can't let that happen.

"You are strong," it says. *"Far stronger than your duplicate. But your time is running out."*

The ships are closing in fast.

"The Herald is already at work. This may be your final chance," it says. *"Open your mind. Let me in."*

But I can't.

"Then you have lost," it says. *"You have lost everything."*

The lead Skelton warship fires a blast near Makeshift 2. His scream pierces the air as he falls. He's hurt, clutching his leg!

Images of my Makeshift cross my mind. He's dead now—a petrified statue—because of me. Because I failed to act when I needed to. I swore I wouldn't let anyone get hurt because of me again.

Dad 2's words echo in my mind: *being a hero is about sacrifice, no matter how painful the consequences may be.*

I know what I've got to do.

I close my eyes.

"Give me the power," I say. *"All of it. Now."*

"Yes!" the Orb exclaims.

I relax my mind and feel a strange sensation running through my body. It's like my cells are opening up—unlocking—filling with incredible energy. Suddenly, I feel super-charged. Electric. Dominant.

The only other time I felt like this was when I was inside the mind of... of... Meta-Taker!

"Am... am I a Meta 4?"

"You are all-powerful," the Orb says. *"You can call it whatever you wish."*

So, if I'm like Meta-Taker, then that means I can duplicate the powers of other Metas! Is that why he told me I could...

Holy. Freaking. Cow!

"How do I do it?" I ask quickly.

"It's simple. You just reach out and take it," the Orb says.

I close my eyes and push out with my mind. But instead of negating Grace 2's powers, this time I copy it, reproduce it, and pull it back into my body.

"Elliott, what are you doing?" Grace 2 says. "Stop twisting, you're going to—Elliott!"

I break loose from their grip and start freefalling.

For a second, I'm terrified. Visions of splattering on

the ground fill my brain. But then, I extend my arms and think 'FLY.'

And suddenly, I stop my descent.

I'm... floating?

I... I did it!

"Hey," Grace says. "How'd you do that?"

"Tell you later," I say. Suddenly, I remember Meta-Taker's profile. There was a part about him being able to duplicate the powers of more than one Meta of the same power type. "But right now, I'm going to need your power too." I reach out and copy Grace's flying ability as well. I can feel their powers multiplying inside of me. "Look, I've got to stop the Herald. Do your best to get rid of these Skelton. And please, don't get killed."

"Elliott," Grace says, "wait a—"

But before she can finish, I'm gone.

The wind snaps against my face as I fly through the sky under my own power. It kind of feels like swimming, where the water you displace weighs more than you do, keeping you afloat. But instead of water, I'm being buoyed by air molecules, and there's no chlorine stinging my eyes.

A few Skelton warships break formation and get on my tail, but with the flight powers of both Glory Girls, I'm way too fast for them. After a few seconds, they fall behind and give up. I'm guessing I've dropped completely off their radars.

I make my way back to Keystone City where there's

not a Skelton in sight. The combined powers of the Freedom Force did a great job pulling the shapeshifters away from the city, but there's tons of damage. Unfortunately, I can't clean it up now, because I'm here to pick up something else—the Herald's fiery trail.

Fortunately, it's still blazing strong.

I take off, following its path.

"Wait, there are no Meta's here," the Orb says. *"The city is vulnerable."*

"So?"

"So, now is a good time to begin your reign," it says. *"To take command of your lowly subjects and rule."*

"Yes, good point."

Wait a minute! What did I just say?

Why would I think that? The Orb is messing with me. And besides, that's crazy talk. I don't want to rule anything! Right?

"Stop it! Get out of my head!"

"Remarkably, you are still holding back," it says. *"Trust me and let go."*

I feel the Orb burrowing into my brain. Somehow, I've got to keep it in line. I can't let it take me over. I've got a job to do.

I'm over the west coast when I notice something disturbing—there's a second blazing pathway. That can only mean one thing, the Herald's made two rotations around Earth already!

I vividly recall what I saw him do to Protaraan,

circling the doomed planet over and over again until he left a signal in the form of a bright, fiery atom which was visible from any point in the universe.

A signal for Ravager to come and feed.

I switch to the new trail and kick into overdrive.

I'm really motoring now when I notice a strangely familiar set of islands dotting the ocean below.

And that's when I see him, a bright fireball cruising through the sky.

"Halt!" I yell.

The Herald peers over his shoulder and smirks. Then, he stops on a dime mid-flight, and I go shooting past. Not exactly the heroic entrance I was hoping for.

"Little hero," he says. "You have come for more punishment."

I manage to put on the brakes and head back towards the villain. During our last encounter I didn't have nearly enough power to take him down. But this time it's going to be different. "This ends now," I say.

Just then, I notice something is wrong. I'm sinking. Lowering in the sky.

"Are you sure about that?" the Herald says amused.

"What's happening?"

"You did not store enough power. And you have drifted too far from your power source," the Orb says. *"You have lost your ability to—"*

Oh. No.

Suddenly, I drop like an anchor.

"Take his power!" the Orb yells.

But I can't focus. I'm plunging towards the ocean from thousands of feet in the air! From this height I'm gonna hit the water and scatter into a million pieces! I can't breathe! I feel like I'm passing out!

Then, my momentum stops.

How?

Drops of water pitter onto my face and my entire backside feels wet. I look down and realize I'm being held up by a giant plume of water.

Not again.

Suddenly, I'm lifted into the air by a green-caped man with a dragon emblem on his chest. "So, we meet again," Green Dragon says.

The Rising Suns!

"Listen," I say. "Thanks for the lift, but I really don't have time to fight you right now."

"We are not here to fight," Zen says, suddenly appearing beside us. "From our last encounter, I was able to share everything I discovered inside your mind. We apologize for before, isn't that right, Green Dragon?"

"Yes," Green Dragon says begrudgingly. "I... apologize. We now know that you are who you claim to be. And this man of fire is our joint enemy. We are here to help you."

I turn to see the Herald holding off Tsunami, Silent Samurai, and Fight Master. And then I realize with the Rising Suns here, I have more powers I can borrow.

"A lot has changed since the last time we met," I say. "And the best way you can help me is by sticking around for a while."

I close my eyes and pull in Zen's Meta 3 psychic abilities, Green Dragon's Meta 3 super-strength, and Tsunami's Meta 3 energy manipulation. Then, I grab their powers of flight.

Now, it's showtime.

I pull away from Green Dragon and fly over to the Herald.

"Little hero," the Herald says. "You have returned. Have you sorted out your problem?"

"Nope," I say coldly, "you're still here."

He smiles. "Still with the sharp tongue, I see. I think it is high time I rip it out." Then, he extends his arms and sends a blast of fire my way.

I use Tsunami's powers and block it with a wave of water, then I push it back towards him using Green Dragon's strength, dousing him in ocean water. The Herald flickers out for a moment, and then flames back on.

"You are stronger," he says. "But not strong enough." Suddenly, he erupts into a bright ball of fire, blinding me. The heat is so intense it feels like my skin is melting! He's trying to vaporize me!

"Now," the Orb says, *"negate his power permanently!"*

I want to do it, but something tells me it's not the right move. Instead, I tap into Zen's psychic power and reach into the Herald's mind.

A series of images flash before me: A green world with yellow, puffy clouds. An image of a pointy-eared woman. Children playing.

"What are you doing?" the Herald cries. "Stop!"

This is incredible! I'm seeing things exactly as the Herald saw them! He's inside a space shuttle drifting into a nebulous, green mist. He's pushing commands on a bomb. But then, his ship is pulled apart around him. He's trapped inside a... a cocoon? Then, he's bathed in fire...

No freaking way! I pull out of his head.

"You tried to destroy Ravager," I say.

He looks at me angrily. "Yes," he says, powering down. "Once upon a time."

"But I don't understand. If you wanted him dead, then why are you helping him destroy other planets?"

"It is... complicated," he says, putting his head in his hands.

"Try me," I say.

"Once I was a scientist," he begins, "an astrologer, who made a remarkable, yet fateful discovery. There were holes in the universe where my ancestors had mapped planets. It seemed as if entire worlds on the far side of the galaxy had disappeared. I did not understand how this could be possible, so I brought my discovery to the Federation, but they did not care. With the ongoing wars, they said they had higher concerns than my lost worlds. But I knew something was wrong."

The Rising Suns surround the Herald, but I raise my hand, stopping them from attacking. "Go on," I say.

"I knew what was happening could not be natural. Something was causing it to happen. I studied the phenomenon for years, until one day, my equipment caught the perpetrator in the act. It was a strange, undefined mist that was swallowing planets whole, and then destroying them. I knew if this cosmic predator was not dealt with, one day it would come for my world, my family, my children."

A fiery tear streams down his face.

"I built a nuclear warhead and said goodbye to my loved ones. I knew I would never see them again. Years passed before I finally came upon the monster, descending upon a small planet in the Oberon system. As I watched it in its ephemeral form, I realized my weapon was useless to destroy it. At least, until it solidified. So, I flew into its center and waited. But, as you saw, I did not destroy it, it destroyed me."

"What happened?" I ask.

"It transformed me," he says, "into this. A servant to hunt habitable worlds for it to consume."

"But why?" I ask. "Why are you doing this?"

"Because, it made me a bargain I could not refuse. In exchange for my service, it offered to spare my world—to save my family."

"But you helped it murder billions."

"Yes," he says, looking down. "I have not thought of

my family for a long time. I saved them, but in the process destroyed many, many others. I... I have lost sight of what matters most. Life. All life."

"Destroy him!" the Orb says.

My fingers twitch and I feel the urge to take all his powers away. To punish him for what he's done, but I can't.

I need him.

"Look, I know what it's like when you're willing to do anything to save your family," I say, "but with the decisions you've made, you've only let them down. You've let yourself down. This is your chance, maybe your only chance to redeem yourself and do what's right. You've got to help me destroy Ravager before he comes to Earth. You have to help me save billions of lives. Do you understand?"

He hesitates for a moment, and then says, "Yes, I understand."

Suddenly, the sky darkens, like someone threw a blanket over the sun.

"But I am afraid it is too late."

Meta Profile

Name: Ravager
Role: Cosmic Entity Status: Active

VITALS:

Race: Inapplicable
Real Name: Inapplicable
Height: Unlimited
Weight: Incalculable
Eye Color: Inapplicable
Hair Color: Inapplicable

META POWERS:

Class: Inapplicable
Power Level: Inapplicable

- A cosmic predator that consumes habitable planets to satiate its endless hunger
- Crosses the multiverse as a shapeless mist

CHARACTERISTICS:

Combat	Inapplicable
Durability	Inapplicable
Leadership	Inapplicable
Strategy	Inapplicable
Willpower	Inapplicable

FOURTEEN

I FACE THE ULTIMATE EVIL

Under a blackened sky, the first tendrils of a menacing green fog descend slowly towards Earth.

My nightmare has come true.

Ravager is here.

"What is happening?" Tsunami asks.

"Just the end of the world," I answer cryptically, hypnotized by what's unfolding before my eyes.

The green cloud rolls in thick and fluffy, almost inviting. But that couldn't be further from the truth.

While I've had nightmares about Ravager attacking Earth before, the sheer terror I'm feeling at this moment is more intense than I ever imagined. As Ravager fills the sky, it dawns on me we're only occupying one tiny section of the globe. If it can swallow entire planets, it must be absolutely huge!

How am I ever going to find its brain? It's going to be impossible—like finding a needle in a haystack. I mean, it could take years! Clearly, I don't have that luxury. And besides, how does a creature made of mist even have a brain?

Suddenly, warning bells go off in my head, and a million reasons why I shouldn't trust the Watcher's advice come to mind. First off, he's batty. Second, Ravager is his child. I mean, does he really want to off his own kid? Third, he hates me. After all, I have the Orb of Oblivion, the only weapon rumored to be capable of taking down his precious Ravager.

Maybe he's sending me to dig my own grave.

Something tells me he'll get his wish.

Hazy, green waves drift past my face and I gag. Yuck, this stuff smells like rotten eggs. Then, I notice something strange. The wispy green particles are covered with small, shiny flecks. At first, they look like they're falling alongside it, like snowflakes from the sky. But then I realize the flecks are somehow attached to the green mist, riding down with it.

That's weird.

"Little h—," the Herald starts but then stops himself. "Epic Zero, I hope you understand the impossible odds before us. I have seen countless others attempt to stop Ravager. Scientists. Soldiers. Superheroes. All have tried, and all have perished. What makes you think we are capable of succeeding where others have failed?"

"Because I have this."

I watch the Herald's eyes widen as I hold out the Orb of Oblivion. "So, it is real," he whispers.

"Yes," I say, "and if we're going to use it, I need you to take me to Ravager's brain. That is, if it actually has a brain."

"It does," he says. "I can take you there. But I fear the journey will be treacherous. We will need to intercept the beast in the harshness of space. You will not survive."

"That's not a problem," I say. And then I concentrate hard, tapping into the Herald's power, copying every iota possible. As I draw in his abilities, I can feel my cells expanding, crackling with energy.

And then I burst into flames.

"Tsunami, put him out!" Fight Master cries.

"No, it's okay," I say quickly. "I'm not hurt. I've simply duplicated the Herald's power. Now I must go and slay the dragon."

Green Dragon raises an eyebrow.

"Sorry," I say. "It's just an expression. What I mean is it's time for me to destroy Ravager before he destroys us."

"Epic Zero," Zen says, "the fate of mankind is in your hands. Good luck."

"Thanks," I say, swallowing hard. Talk about pressure! This is it. There's no turning back now. I take a deep breath and say, "Let's do this."

Without a word, the Herald takes off. He's fast, but this time I'm right there with him.

The Herald cuts through the fog like a flaming knife, leaving a blazing trail in his wake. Suddenly, I realize we're flying straight through Ravager's body. It's like he's a ghost, like he's not really there. I only wish that were true.

One thing that is there though, are those shiny flecks. They're everywhere, pelting lightly against my face. What are they?

"I was wondering the same thing," the Orb says. *"I sense a cosmic energy about them. Something familiar."*

"For such a know-it-all, you sure don't know much," I say.

"Don't worry, I'll figure it out," it says. *"Speaking of 'knowing,' you do know what to do once we reach Ravager's brain, right?"*

"Yes, I'm going to blow you up."

"Wrong," it says. *"When we reach Ravager's brain, we will take control of Ravager. After we master the beast, the entire multiverse will bow before us. Imagine the power you'll have. Imagine the respect you will earn."*

Yes, that would be something, wouldn't it? I'd be unstoppable! I can just see Grace's face when I swing by the Waystation with Ravager on a leash. Boy, will she be sur—

"Hey!" I shout, "Get lost!"

The Herald stops. "Excuse me?"

"Sorry," I say, embarrassed. "Just having a private

conversation." Suddenly, I realize we've left Earth's atmosphere altogether. We're floating in space! I'm floating in space! But my excitement is short-lived when I catch full sight of Ravager.

It's like there's no end in sight. The creature extends from deep space all the way to Earth! And he's covered half the globe already! We're running out of time!

"Where's the brain?" I say, panicked. I'm looking around for something, anything, but there's nothing. "We need to get there! Now!"

"But we are here," the Herald says. "Look."

I follow his outstretched hand, which is pointing to a cloudy area that is subtlety darker than the rest. It's the size of a football field, expanding and contracting.

"That's the brain?" I ask.

"Yes," he says. "But it is in transient form. If you try to destroy it now, its molecules will simply scatter and reform again. If you want to ensure its demise, you must wait until it solidifies."

"Okay," I say. "So, when will that happen?"

"When it fully swallows your planet."

"Whoa," I say. "So, you're saying I need to wait for it to start pulverizing Earth before I can destroy it? I can't let that happen. It'll kill billions!"

"That," the Herald says, "is the only way."

Suddenly, there's a THUNDEROUS BOOM.

"What's that?" I ask.

"Master!" the Herald screams.

The brain shakes violently and out comes something that is not so much a voice, but a rumble.

"YOU BETRAYED ME."

"No, Master," the Herald says. "I was just... bringing this boy here... to witness your mighty power."

"DO YOU TAKE ME FOR A FOOL? THIS IS NO ORDINARY BOY. HE IS THE ORB MASTER. AND YOU BROUGHT HIM HERE TO DESTROY ME."

"Now!" the Herald screams. "Destroy it now!"

I reach into my mind to activate the Orb's power, when—

"Wait!" the Orb says. *"It's not solid. It won't work."*

I hesitate. The Orb is right. Based on what the Herald told me, using the Orb's power now wouldn't do any good.

"FOR OVER A CENTURY YOU HAVE ACTED AS MY LOYAL SUBJECT. BUT NOW YOU HAVE CONSPIRED AGAINST ME. OUR BARGAIN IS TERMINATED. YOUR WORLD WILL BE RAVAGED AND NOW YOU WILL BE PUNISHED!"

"No!" the Herald cries, dropping into a begging position. "I'm sorry, Master! Please, let me make it up to—"

Just then, the Herald's fire is extinguished.

For the first time, I see the man beneath the flames—his skin is white, his eyes are gold. He stares at me desperately and then clutches his throat.

He can't breathe! Without his powers he can't breathe in space!

"Herald!" I cry, moving towards him, but the green mist between us thickens, forming a barrier. I try pushing through it, but the fog has solidified! I can't break through! I've lost sight of him.

Just then, the fog dissipates, and as it creeps away I see the Herald's body floating before me. Limp. Lifeless.

He's gone.

Suddenly, I panic. My power source is gone!

"Don't worry," the Orb says, *"this time you've stored enough juice to last a while. But don't dilly-dally."*

That's a relief. But as the Herald hovers there, all I'm thinking is here's another senseless death. Another life I'm responsible for. My blood is boiling. All I want is to destroy Ravager—to end this nightmare. But how?

"I REQUIRE A NEW HERALD."

"You're going to need more than that," I say, "after I blow you into a gazillion pieces."

"HOW ABOUT YOU?"

"What?"

"YOU ARE STRONG. DETERMINED. I WILL TAKE YOU AS MY HERALD, AND IN EXCHANGE I WILL SPARE YOUR WORLD."

"Um, is that a joke?"

"SERVE AS MY HERALD. SCOUT THE MULTIVERSE TO FIND HABITABLE PLANETS

TO SATIATE MY HUNGER. HELP ME, AND YOUR WORLD, AND ALL OF THOSE YOU LOVE, WILL LIVE. THE OFFER HAS BEEN MADE, THE FINAL DECISION IS YOURS."

FIFTEEN

I DETERMINE THE FATE OF EVERYTHING

My head is spinning.

Ravager just offered Earth a get-out-of-jail-free card. There's just one catch. To cash it in, I need to become his new Herald.

My gut tells me to say, 'thanks but no thanks.'

But my head tells me it may be an offer I can't refuse.

I mean, everything I've done up to this point has been for the sole purpose of preventing Ravager from eating Earth. All of my adventures flash through my mind: getting captured by the Rising Suns, traveling through wormholes to another universe, wrestling Elliott 2 on Watcher World, fighting with the second Orb of

Oblivion. It's been an insane whirlwind.

Now, if I just say 'yes' the whole threat is neutralized. My family will be spared. My friends on the Freedom Force will survive. My planet will be left alone. It's an amazing deal.

But not for everyone.

I think about my old friends on the Zodiac: Gemini, Taurus, Aries, Sagittarius, Pisces, and Scorpio. They're all orphans, the last of their kind, all because of Ravager's hunger pains.

Then, my mind turns to Grace 2 and her family. Their world won't be safe either. One day, Ravager will come for them too.

I remember how sad the Herald looked when I confronted him about his actions. Even though he thought he was doing the right thing, he knew he was as guilty as Ravager in the slaughtering of billions.

I can't do that.

I could never do that.

"Are you nuts?" the Orb says. *"This is the chance of a lifetime."*

"No, I don't think—"

"Listen, dummy," it interjects. *"This is your one chance to save everyone you care about. I know you think you can use me to blow that monster up, but what if it doesn't work? You'll be responsible for what happens next. Don't doom everyone you love because of some silly moral code. Step up and show them you're the hero you were meant to be."*

Maybe the Orb is right. If I screw it up, Earth is lost. Maybe this is my one shot to save my planet. Plus, who knows what's going to happen with the multiverse collapsing.

But if I become the new Herald, I'll be responsible for hurting so many innocent people. I... I don't know what to do. How come I'm always stuck making these decisions? I'm sure Dad or Mom would know what to do. I bet even Dog-Gone could make the call better than me.

"DECIDE, EARTHLING!" Ravager rumbles.

"Do it!" the Orb says. *"Before it's too late!"*

I rub my thumb along the smooth surface of the Orb. Great, so here I've got the most powerful weapon in the universe, but no clue how to use it. The Watcher said to take the Orb to the brain of Ravager, and then blow it up. He didn't provide any instructions after that.

But Ravager is a trail of gas fumes right now. According to the Herald, it needs to be in solid form for me to do any real damage. The last time I saw it turn solid was when it cracked Protaraan like a walnut, extracting all of its life energy for nourishment. If I wait for it to do the same to Earth, it could destroy it.

So, how am I going to blow it up?

Hang on.

Blow. It. Up?

Maybe I'm looking at this the wrong way.

Okay, so I've got the Orb of Oblivion—the cosmic parasite that specializes in one thing other than rudeness—mind control. And for all his gaseous grossness, Ravager clearly has a brain—a mind of its own.

I know what to do.

"*Orb,*" I command, "*make Ravager retreat.*"

"*What?*" the Orb says. "*I'll do no such thing.*"

"Oh, yes you—"

"EARTHLING," Ravager bellows, regaining my attention. "WHAT IS YOUR DECISION?"

Really? Like it couldn't have waited another second. I could try stalling for more time, but I've got a feeling that isn't gonna work. I've got no choice. Here goes nothing. "Thanks for the generous offer," I answer. "But I'd rather die an epic failure than ever be a herald for you!"

"THEN THE FATE OF YOUR WORLD IS SEALED."

Suddenly, Ravager shifts towards Earth in double time! A feeling of dread washes over me, but there's no time to second guess myself. I've made my decision and now I've got to get down to business!

"*Orb!*" I command. "*Make Ravager retreat!*"

"*No w*—"

"*Enough!*" I demand. "*You are the Orb and I am the Orb Master! You will do as I say! NOW!*"

I recall the Orb telling me it hid part of itself from Elliott 2. That's how it was able to transfer to me. Somehow, it never allowed the other Elliott to take it over completely. But for this job I'm going to need the Orb—the whole Orb.

I drive deep into the Orb's conscious.

The Orb screams. It pushes back.

But I'm too strong.

I dig deeper.

It squirms, trying to avoid my pressure.

But I won't be denied.

I surround it. Trap it. Seize it.

And then, I break its will.

I feel the Orb yield. Open itself up.

And I take it all.

The Orb is mine. Fully mine.

Then, I focus my energy on one thought.

BRING BACK RAVAGER.

A massive wave of orange energy explodes out of the Orb and grabs hold of the beast, wrapping around its vaporous middle, cinching tight. Ravager lurches forward, pulling me with it. But I yank back hard, dragging the monster backward.

Ravager SCREAMS—an other-worldly primal scream—like a cranky child pulled from his highchair before finishing his meal. The cosmic monster loses its grip on Earth, its tendrils flailing. But it's not going down without a fight. It fires a shockwave back through the Orb, stunning me.

But I hold firm.

I pull harder, reeling it in like a fish. When I finally get it clear of Earth's atmosphere, I begin part two of my plan. I remember Dad 2's Distorter. How it made people think something was there, even when it wasn't. And I know what I need to do.

"Orb," I command. *"Trick Ravager into thinking he's consuming a habitable planet."*

"Yes, master," the Orb responds.

Suddenly, Ravager's wispy molecules blow up and out, forming a gigantic balloon shape, larger than Earth. Ravager has wrapped itself around the imaginary planet.

Now, it's time to end this once and for all.

"D-Don't... do it," the Orb begs. *"Please..."*

What? How is the Orb still resisting me?

"No dice," I say.

Suddenly, Ravager turns solid. It thinks it's going to crush the imaginary planet.

This is my chance.

"You'll destroy Earth, you fool," the Orb says. *"You're too close. It'll be wiped out in the explosion."*

Oh, jeez! I didn't think of that.

And then—

"Do not listen to it," comes a familiar voice. "It is manipulating you. Act now."

"But what about Earth?" I say.

"We will protect it," comes another voice. "All of it."

"No!" the Orb says. *"That's not possible! You're dead! You're both dead!"*

"Act now!" urges the first voice.

"Orb," I command, *"get into the sphere. All of you."*

I feel a rush as the Orb of Oblivion leaves my body

and enters the sphere in my hand.

Then, I grip the sphere tight and hurl it as hard as I can at Ravager.

With incredible velocity, the Orb flies through the vacuum of space, straight and true.

But as it reaches Ravager, something amazing happens. Millions of those strange, tiny flecks leave Ravager's body, forming a barrier in front of Earth.

"Now," comes the second voice, bringing me back to reality. "Do it now!"

I reach out and connect to the Orb of Oblivion. And then I make one final command.

DETONATE!

As the massive explosion begins, I'm covered by tiny flecks of light.

And then everything goes black.

***

It's dark. At first, I think someone's turned out the lights, but then I realize my eyes are closed. My whole body is sore. It feels like I've been hit by a Mack truck. How long have I been lying here? Am I dead?

I open my eyes, expecting to see either angels or devils. What I find instead is pretty darn close, because standing on opposite sides of the bed are two familiar faces.

Order and Chaos.

I shoot up. "B-But you're dead?" I say. "I saw you both killed on Arena World."

Order smiles, his teeth still perfectly straight. "One cannot kill the very fabric of the universe. Instead, let us say we were temporarily displaced."

I try to make a sense of what he's saying when suddenly it all clicks. Those tiny flecks attached to Ravager. Those voices I heard in my head. All of those shiny particles that protected Earth.

"So, wait a minute," I say. "Those tiny flecks on Ravager? That was you guys?"

Chaos brushes some lint off his leather jacket. "Yes. And I can assure you having a simple thought when you are scattered across the galaxy is nearly impossible. So, we were glad you finally arrived when you did. You followed our plan to a tee."

"Plan?" I say. "What plan?"

"Our plan to restore our power," Order says. "After your colleague surprised us on Arena World we were dispersed into millions of atoms. Together, we gravitated to the strongest source of cosmic energy we could find—Ravager. We clung to the monster, but being so weak, we did not have the power to reassemble ourselves. To do so, we required a large influx of cosmic energy."

"As you surely noticed," Chaos continues, "without my brother and I to manage the rules of the multiverse, things started to go awry. We knew we had to act quickly, otherwise, everything we had built over an eternity would be undone in the blink of an eye. And while I like disorder, I like it on my terms. So, we merged what little strength we had, and focused our combined power to redirect Ravager away from his diversions, and towards your planet."

"What?" I say. "You mean Ravager coming to Earth was your fault?"

"Yes," Order says. "Because we needed you, Orb Master. With the threat of Ravager looming, we hoped you would realize the need for an Orb of Oblivion. And given your exposure to the duplicate heroes of Earth 2, it would only be natural for you to find your way to their world. If you successfully recovered the second Orb, we knew you had a chance to destroy Ravager, which would release enough cosmic energy for us to restore ourselves to our proper forms."

"So, good job, kid," Chaos says.

"And the Orb?" I ask, bracing myself for the answer. The Orb has been stuck to me like Velcro. Every time I think I'm done with it, it comes back with a vengeance.

"It is gone," Order says. "You have nothing to fear. The Orb of Oblivion, all Orbs of Oblivion, are no more."

I feel a tremendous sense of relief. Finally!

But then I feel angry. I mean, this whole time I was just a puppet in their plan. Earth was just a chip in their game. This whole thing was a scheme to get me to free them. I feel like I'm going to explode.

"Do not be upset with us," Order says, reading my

expression. "Your actions have saved what is left of the multiverse. The 'Blur,' as you call it, has ended. Structure and discipline have returned."

"For the moment," Chaos says with a sneer in his voice.

"Indeed," Order says. "And your world is safe. We thought it a fitting reward for all you have accomplished. And we have also agreed to bestow upon you a gift."

"Reluctantly," Chaos adds.

"Gift? What gift?"

"You will receive it when the appropriate time comes," Order says. "Farewell, Elliott Harkness, you have done well. You are truly a hero. Perhaps the best of your kind."

"Wait!" I say. "What's this g—"

But then, everything vanishes.

EPILOGUE

IT'S HARD TO BELIEVE...

I never thought I'd live to see two genius rats debate over the stability of unstable molecules. But I guess it's better than the alternative.

Since Order and Chaos dumped me back on the Waystation, I've been trying to sort through everything that's happened. I can't believe they played me like the thimble in their galactic game of monopoly. They were using me the whole time, I just didn't know it.

The odds of me beating Ravager must have been a quad-trillion-billion to one. Yet somehow, I got it done. Now that I saved Earth and stopped the Blur, I hope I never see those two cosmic clowns again.

So, sitting in the lab watching both TechnocRat's go back and forth over the technical fitness of the Jump Ship is a welcome distraction. And speaking of distractions, the combined Freedom Force successfully turned back the Skelton invaders, but Keystone City looks like a war zone. Fortunately, no civilians were seriously hurt. I don't think the Skelton can say the same.

According to TechnocRat 2's readings, Earth 2 is still there, which I'm thankful for. After all, Grace 2 just got her dad back and I'd hate for her to lose him again. Plus, they get a chance to rebuild their world without the threat of Elliott 2.

I wonder what he and the Watcher have been up to. I can just see them sitting around a campfire exchanging ghost stories over s'mores. Of course, Dog-Gone 2 probably stole all the marshmallows.

My Dog-Gone is lying by my side. I think he's forgiven me for sneaking off without him to chase after the Herald. When I materialized in the Galley, he pounced on me, licking my face until I nearly drowned in slobber. Then, he demanded ten doggie treats which I was more than happy to pay up.

I catch Grace 2's gaze and she smiles back nervously. I can tell she's anxious about making it home. While all the threats have been neutralized, there's still the risk the Jump Ship won't work. Traveling by wormhole was crazier, but more reliable with Wind Walker doing the driving.

You know, I never did hear back from Wind Walker. The worry on his face as he left was haunting. I hope he's okay, but I've got a funny feeling he's in trouble.

Suddenly, TechnocRat 2 puts down a wrench and declares, "The Jump Ship is officially operational."

Mom 2 turns to my mom and says, "Well, I guess this is it."

They hug and Mom says, "It was a pleasure working with you. We'll have to do this again sometime."

Mom 2 smiles and says, "Yes, but next time why don't you visit us. Hopefully, under less dire circumstances."

"Deal," Mom says.

The rest of the heroes all say their goodbyes.

"You know," Grace says to Grace 2, "I've got to admit, I look pretty good as a brunette."

"And I'm thinking of going blond," Grace 2 says, hugging my sister. "Take care of that brother of yours."

"I'll keep an eye on him," Grace says, putting her hand on my shoulder. "But I think he's proven he can take care of himself."

Grace 2 gives me a big hug. "The next time you're in town, give me advance notice so I can warn everyone else. See you soon?"

"You can count on it," I say. "Thanks for all of your help. And say hi to your dad for me. Let him know he ended up helping me out in a big way."

She smiles. "Will do."

The Freedom Force 2 step into the Jump Ship.

"Captain?" TechnocRat 2 says.

"Ready," Dad says, lifting the Jump Ship into the air.

TechnocRat scrambles up onto Dad's shoulder. "Are you certain you've properly factored the difference in atmospheric pressure of—"

"—being inside a cabin in outer space?" TechnocRat 2 finishes. "The answer for the five hundredth time is 'yes!' Now, my dear Captain, if you will do the honors."

The heroes inside the Jump Ship grab on to the newly installed safety rails—a welcome addition added by my TechnocRat.

Grace 2 waves at me.

"Here comes the heater," Dad says. And then he rears back and launches the Jump Ship.

I cover my eyes. This better work!

Fortunately, the bubble vanishes before it hits the far wall. Hooray for unstable molecules!

"I hope he got those calculations right," TechnocRat mutters. "Why, I've never met such a stubborn rat in all my life!"

We all laugh.

"I say we celebrate with some jelly doughnuts in the Galley," Blue Bolt suggests.

"And peanut butter and banana sandwiches," Shadow Hawk adds.

"I'm in!" Grace says.

The heroes begin to exit, but I can't move! For some reason, I can't lift my feet. It's like I'm stuck to the ground. What's going on?

"Elliott," Dad says. "Aren't you coming?"

Something tells me not to mention what's happening. I have this strange urge to stay here. "No, you guys go ahead," I say. "I'll be there in a minute. Promise."

"Okay," Mom says. "We'll see you in a bit."

After they leave, I'm suddenly able to move again. But instead of heading for the door, I find myself walking to the back of the lab.

To the back corner.

To Makeshift.

Through all of this craziness, he's been stuck here hooked up to all of those wires and monitors, like a permanent monument of my failure.

"I'm so sorry, old buddy," I say. "But if you knew what I did, maybe you'd be proud of me."

I lay my hand on his cold, solid arm when all of a sudden a strange orange energy flows out of my fingertips.

What's going on?

It runs up Makeshift's body and down the other side.

And then, before my eyes, he transforms from a cold, petrified statue, back to warm flesh-and-blood!

I catch him as he collapses to his knees.

"Makeshift? You're alive!"

"What h-happened?" he asks. "Elliott?"

I don't have a ready answer. And then I remember.

The gift!

I'm suddenly overwhelmed with emotion. Tears

stream down my cheeks.

"Hey, buddy," Makeshift says. "Are you okay?"

"Never been better," I say, wiping my eyes.

"Man, I'm starving," he says. "Got anything to eat?"

Good old Makeshift.

"Plenty," I say, helping him to his feet. "Let's head down to the Galley. There are some old friends and a furry food partner who are dying to see you."

As we walk out, I look through the nearest porthole, into the starry expanse of space and whisper, "Thanks."

And a million stars twinkle at once.

EPIC ZERO 4 IS AVAILABLE NOW!

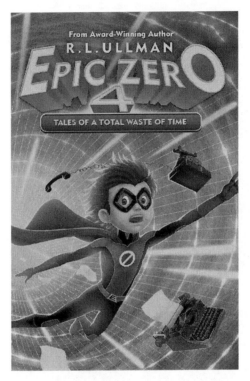

Elliott realizes a time-trotting troublemaker has gone into the past and changed everything! In order to fix the present, Elliott must follow him back in time. But can Elliott make things right without destroying the future?

**Get Epic Zero 4:
Tales of a Total Waste of Time today!**

YOU CAN MAKE A BIG DIFFERENCE

Calling all heroes! I need your help to get Epic Zero 3 in front of more readers.

Reviews are extremely helpful in getting attention for my books. I wish I had the marketing muscle of the major publishers, but instead, I have something far more valuable, loyal readers, just like you! Your generosity in providing an honest review will help bring this book to the attention of more readers.

So, if you've enjoyed this book, I would be very grateful if you could spare a minute to leave a review on the book's Amazon page.

Thanks for your support!

R.L. Ullman

META POWERS GLOSSARY

FROM THE META MONITOR:

There are nine known Meta power classifications. These classifications have been established to simplify Meta identification and provide a quick framework to understand a Meta's potential powers and capabilities. **Note:** Metas can possess powers in more than one classification. In addition, Metas can evolve over time in both the powers they express, as well as the effectiveness of their powers.

Due to the wide range of Meta abilities, superpowers have been further segmented into power levels. Power levels differ across Meta power classifications. In general, the following power levels have been established:

- Meta 0: Displays no Meta power.
- Meta 1: Displays limited Meta power.
- Meta 2: Displays considerable Meta power.
- Meta 3: Displays extreme Meta power.

The following is a brief overview of the nine Meta power classifications.

ENERGY MANIPULATION:

Energy Manipulation is the ability to generate, shape, or act as a conduit, for various forms of energy. Energy

Manipulators can control energy by focusing or redirecting energy towards a specific target or shaping/reshaping energy for a specific task. Energy Manipulators are often impervious to the forms of energy they can manipulate.

Examples of the types of energies utilized by Energy Manipulators include, but are not limited to:

- Atomic
- Chemical
- Cosmic
- Electricity
- Gravity
- Heat
- Light
- Magnetic
- Sound
- Space
- Time

Note: the fundamental difference between an Energy Manipulator and a Meta-morph with Energy Manipulation capability is that an Energy Manipulator does not change their physical or molecular state to either generate or transfer energy (see META-MORPH).

FLIGHT:

Flight is the ability to fly, glide, or levitate above the Earth's surface without the use of an external source (e.g. jetpack). Flight can be accomplished through a variety of methods, these include, but are not limited to:

- Reversing the force of gravity
- Riding air currents
- Using planetary magnetic fields
- Wings

Metas exhibiting Flight can range from barely sustaining flight a few feet off the ground to reaching the far limits of outer space.

Often, Metas with Flight ability also display the complementary ability of Super-Speed. However, it can be difficult to decipher if Super-Speed is a Meta power in its own right or is simply a function of combining the Meta's Flight ability with the Earth's natural gravitational force.

MAGIC:

Magic is the ability to display a wide variety of Meta abilities by channeling the powers of a secondary magical or mystical source. Known secondary sources of Magic powers include, but are not limited to:

- Alien lifeforms
- Dark arts
- Demonic forces
- Departed souls
- Mystical spirits

Typically, the forces of Magic are channeled through an enchanted object. Known magical, enchanted objects include:

- Amulets
- Books
- Cloaks
- Gemstones
- Wands
- Weapons

Some Magicians can transport themselves into the mystical realm of their magical source. They may also have the ability to transport others into and out of these realms as well.

Note: the fundamental difference between a Magician and an Energy Manipulator is that a Magician typically channels their powers from a mystical source that likely requires the use of an enchanted object to express these powers (see ENERGY MANIPULATOR).

META MANIPULATION:

Meta Manipulation is the ability to duplicate or negate the Meta powers of others. Meta Manipulation is a rare Meta power and can be extremely dangerous if the Meta Manipulator is capable of manipulating the powers of multiple Metas at one time. Meta Manipulators who can manipulate the powers of several Metas at once have been observed to reach Meta 4 power levels.

Based on the unique powers of the Meta Manipulator, it is hypothesized that other abilities could include altering or controlling the powers of others. Despite their tremendous abilities, Meta Manipulators are often unable to generate powers of their own and are limited to manipulating the powers of others. When not utilizing their abilities, Meta Manipulators may be vulnerable to attack.

Note: It has been observed that a Meta Manipulator requires close physical proximity to a Meta target to fully manipulate their power. When fighting a Meta Manipulator, it is advised to stay at a reasonable distance and to attack from long range. Meta Manipulators have been observed manipulating the powers of others over great distances.

META-MORPH:

Meta-morph is the ability to display a wide variety of Meta abilities by "morphing" all, or part, of one's physical form from one state into another. There are two sub-types of Meta-morphs:

- Physical
- Molecular

Physical morphing occurs when a Meta-morph transforms their physical state to express their powers. Physical Meta-morphs typically maintain their human physiology while exhibiting their powers (with the exception of Shapeshifters). Types of Physical morphing include, but are not limited to:

- Invisibility
- Malleability (elasticity/plasticity)
- Physical by-products (silk, toxins, etc…)
- Shapeshifting
- Size changes (larger or smaller)

Molecular morphing occurs when a Meta-morph transforms their molecular state from a normal physical state to a non-physical state to express their powers. Types of Molecular morphing include, but are not limited to:

- Fire
- Ice
- Rock
- Sand
- Steel
- Water

Note: Because Meta-morphs can display abilities that mimic all other Meta power classifications, it can be difficult to properly identify a Meta-morph upon the first encounter. However, it is critical to carefully observe how their powers manifest, and, if it is through Physical or Molecular morphing, you can be certain you are dealing with a Meta-morph.

PSYCHIC:

Psychic is the ability to use one's mind as a weapon. There are two sub-types of Psychics:

- Telepaths
- Telekinetics

Telepathy is the ability to read and influence the thoughts of others. While Telepaths often do not appear to be physically intimidating, their power to penetrate minds can often result in more devastating damage than a physical assault.

Telekinesis is the ability to manipulate physical objects with one's mind. Telekinetics can often move objects with their mind that are much heavier than they could move physically. Many Telekinetics can also make objects move at very high speeds.

Note: Psychics are known to strike from long distances, and in a fight it is advised to incapacitate them as quickly as possible. Psychics often become physically drained from the extended use of their powers.

SUPER-INTELLIGENCE:

Super-Intelligence is the ability to display levels of intelligence above standard genius intellect. Super-Intelligence can manifest in many forms, including, but not limited to:

- Superior analytical ability
- Superior information synthesizing
- Superior learning capacity
- Superior reasoning skills

Note: Super-Intellects continuously push the envelope in the fields of technology, engineering, and weapons development. Super-Intellects are known to invent new approaches to accomplish previously impossible tasks. When dealing with a Super-Intellect, you should be mentally prepared to face challenges that have never been encountered before. In addition, Super-Intellects can come in all shapes and sizes. The most advanced Super-Intellects have originated from non-human creatures.

SUPER-SPEED:

Super-Speed is the ability to display movement at remarkable physical speeds above standard levels of speed. Metas with Super-Speed often exhibit complementary abilities to movement that include, but are not limited to:

- Enhanced endurance
- Phasing through solid objects
- Super-fast reflexes
- Time travel

Note: Metas with Super-Speed often have an equally super metabolism, burning thousands of calories per minute, and requiring them to eat many extra meals a day to maintain consistent energy levels. It has been observed that Metas exhibiting Super-Speed are quick thinkers, making it difficult to keep up with their thought process.

SUPER-STRENGTH:

Super-Strength is the ability to utilize muscles to display remarkable levels of physical strength above expected levels of strength. Metas with Super-Strength can lift or push objects that are well beyond the capability of an average member of their species. Metas exhibiting Super-Strength can range from lifting objects twice their weight to incalculable levels of strength allowing for the movement of planets.

Metas with Super-Strength often exhibit complementary abilities to strength that include, but are not limited to:

- Earthquake generation through stomping
- Enhanced jumping
- Invulnerability
- Shockwave generation through clapping

Note: Metas with Super-Strength may not always possess this strength evenly. Metas with Super-Strength have been observed to demonstrate powers in only one arm or leg.

META PROFILE CHARACTERISTICS

FROM THE META MONITOR:
In addition to having a strong working knowledge of a Meta's powers and capabilities, it is also imperative to understand the key characteristics that form the core of their character. When facing or teaming up with Metas, understanding their key characteristics will help you gain deeper insight into their mentality and strategic potential.

What follows is a brief explanation of the five key characteristics you should become familiar with. **Note**: the data that appears in each Meta profile has been compiled from live field activity.

COMBAT:
The ability to defeat a foe in hand-to-hand combat.

DURABILITY:
The ability to withstand significant wear, pressure, or damage.

LEADERSHIP:
The ability to lead a team of disparate personalities and powers to victory.

STRATEGY:
The ability to find, and successfully exploit, a foe's weakness.

WILLPOWER:
The ability to persevere, despite seemingly insurmountable odds.

GET MORE EPIC FREE!

Don't miss any of the Epic action!

Get a **FREE** copy of
Epic Zero Extra: Tales of a Superhero Screw Up
only at rlullman.com.

ABOUT THE AUTHOR

R.L. Ullman is the bestselling author of the award-winning EPIC ZERO series and the award-winning MONSTER PROBLEMS series. He creates fun, engaging page-turners that captivate the imaginations of kids and adults alike. His original, relatable characters face adventure and adversity that bring out their inner strengths. He's frequently distracted thinking up new stories, and once got lost in his own neighborhood. You can learn more about what R.L. is up to at rlullman.com, and if you see him wandering around your street please point him in the right direction home.

For news, updates, and free stuff, please sign up for the Epic Newsflash at rlullman.com.

ACKNOWLEDGMENTS

Without the support of these brave heroes, I would have been trampled by supervillains before I could bring this series to print. I would like to thank my wife, Lynn (a.k.a. Mrs. Marvelous); my daughter Olivia (a.k.a. Ms. Positivity); and my son Matthew (a.k.a. Captain Creativity). I would also like to thank all of the readers out there who have connected with Elliott and his amazing family. Stay Epic!

Made in the USA
San Bernardino, CA
20 July 2020

75668951R00117